ADVENTURES IN HIRING

MARRIED THIS YEAR BOOK THREE

TRACEY PEDERSEN

DARING ONLINE ADVENTURES

Adventures In Hiring

Copyright © 2017 Tracey Pedersen

PRINT ISBN-13: 978-0-6487909-1-4

This book is dedicated to my ARC team. They saved my life on this book! I'm so grateful to have them on my side!

CONTENTS

ACKNOWLEDGMENT

The people who, again, need the most acknowledgment in the creation of this book are my fabulous readers. I had so much fun including them in book one of this series that I decided to do it again for book three. The submissions for the competition made me laugh, and cry, and I'm so glad I decided to have a second go at including my reader's job interview disasters!

A large number of the things you read about actually happened to readers, and the scene where Emily is pulled over after running a red light actually happened to me only ten days before the book was due to be published. I laughed so hard that night that I knew I had to include it in the story somehow.

My readers are hilarious and I hope I have the chance to do this again in the future. The winners of my competition have characters named after them in this book but for clarity's sake, their names are listed here. I'll leave it up to you to wonder who submitted which idea!

Special thanks goes to these readers (in no particular order):

Kerrie Andrews
Keryth Belvin
Stacy Cook
Lucy Jones
Tiffany Kirven
Athena Kelly
Cindy Honig-Fong
Lacey Waters
Andrea Hilton
Heather

CHAPTER 1

"Nooooo! No. No. No."

Emily clicked back to the start to watch the video again, her mouth open in a silent scream, her eyebrows slammed together. A second later the face of her boss appeared and he repeated his message. "Hi Em. I don't want to alarm you but the directors had a meeting last night and we've decided to press ahead with some radical changes," he paused as he looked into his phone camera. "Immediate changes. At ten o'clock this morning I'm sending a consultant to your branch to work directly with you. We know the strain everyone has been under since the," he coughed, "recent disruption, and we want to fix it for you. Our consultant has years of experience in our industry. He's been the managing director for a very large firm and you and he are going to find us some stellar new staff and make considered decisions about our current ones. I know you're set to travel a bit over the next few months and I'm sure once he's settled, that won't be impacted too much. I've sent you the minutes of the meeting in a separate email and you'll see you've been empowered to make the high level hiring decisions for the next six weeks. We trust you Em, and we're looking forward to great results." He glanced behind his phone and nodded. "Oh. Here's Cooper Jackson, who you'll be working with, by the way."

The camera turned around and a handsome man with surfer-blonde hair grinned at her. "Hi Emily!" he said brightly, followed by a little wave. She groaned again at the sight of that smile.

The camera quickly turned back to her manager, Ed, who continued speaking as he said with his own smile, "We wanted to make sure you didn't just let anyone in the building. One of those incidents this year is enough already, don't you think?" He chuckled to himself and Emily rolled her eyes.

It's not my fault you had an idiot manager here who let the competition into our warehouse!

"Read your email and shoot me back anything I need to know. Thanks Emily, we couldn't have managed these last months without your fabulous work. We're so lucky to have you." He gave a little smile and then his eyes shifted to the screen until he found the stop button. His face froze on her monitor as Emily sat back in her chair.

"Oh Jesus Christ, no!" She was going to have to work side by side with Cooper Jackson. The same Cooper Jackson she'd broken up with nine months ago, after just a few dates. The one she'd hoped never to see again after the way he'd behaved. "What are they bloody thinking?" she said aloud, glancing at her office door to make sure no one could hear. "Ha! Who's going to hear me? We hardly have any staff!"

Simpsons Stationery was lucky to still be in business. A national stationer with a huge client list of franchised stores, they'd recently had to let three important staff members go. The operations manager, the head of accounting and the sales manager had all been terminated on the same day when the board of directors confirmed they'd been involved in price fixing and creating preferential contracts with some suppliers. It wasn't enough that the company now faced a lengthy legal battle to defend itself against the regulator; Emily Pennington had been the one to quietly inform the board of the problem when she'd been handed the proof.

Doing your job well and upholding your own morals were easy when you didn't think about the consequences. What she hadn't known was how the other staff would react when they found out she'd been the one to tell. The last three months had been difficult. The remaining staff had been forced to work long hours to keep the business afloat. Several had resigned and replacing them was now a priority. Those left behind were suspicious of her motives.

Without a site manager, much of the day to day running had fallen on Emily's shoulders. As the most senior manager, she now fielded dozens of interruptions each day, asking about everything from getting sign off to order more toilet paper, to changing courier companies, or hiring casual workers in the warehouse. A consultant to come in and help was a great idea. That person being Cooper Jackson was not!

She glanced at the clock and a horrified expression crossed her face. Quarter to ten! He'll be here any minute!

Why, oh why did I escort the firemen through the site this morning? Why didn't I check my email first thing?

It wouldn't have mattered if she had, he'd have still been on his way.

I might have had time to flee the country!

That thought had hardly registered, when her phone rang. She pushed the speaker button, dread tickling her ribs, "Hello?"

"Emily, there's a Mr Jackson here to see you." She closed her eyes, slid her chair back and put her forehead on the desk. "Emily?" Sasha's voice wafted out of the phone.

"Yes, I'm here. Can you please sign him in and bring him up to my office?"

~

*C*ooper's face was exactly how she remembered it.

His chiselled jaw was clean shaven. His blue eyes sparkled and his trademark grin split his face as he shook her hand. Sasha glanced at Emily, said nothing and slipped out of the door—but not before a backward glance at Cooper's bum. Emily pointed to the chair across from her desk and he settled himself before meeting her eye and smiling again. "I bet you're surprised to see me."

"Not really. Ed did send the video after all."

He doesn't need to know I found out ten minutes ago!

"You know what I mean, Emily. I was surprised to see your name on the staff list."

"Well, it's been a while—"

"Nine months."

"I wasn't counting."

"I might have been."

"Enough!" she raised her hand and frowned at him. "This is never going to work. It's a huge conflict of interest for you to be making decisions about this branch. About me. We need to tell Ed why it's an issue and make other arrangements. He'll have to get someone else to assist you and I'll stay right out of your way."

"Where's the fun in that?" his cheeky grin

surprised her. Anyone else would have agreed and taken immediate steps to sort this situation out. Cooper just relaxed back into his seat and pulled a pen from his shirt pocket. "Chill Emily. I already told Ed we dated a few times. I assured him it wouldn't be a problem for me and he said he was going to email you to check you were okay with it. Didn't he do that?"

She bit her lip and glared at him. He'd taken the wind out of her sails, and her upcoming rant about transparency in the workplace, with his easy answer. If she'd had more than two seconds free this morning she might have read the email that both Ed and, now Cooper, had referred to. Her honesty got the better of her, "I haven't had time to look at the rest of my emails yet. The firemen were here for a site inspection when I arrived, and since we have no health and safety manager, I had to take care of that. Then I signed cheques for accounting, did the final proofs on some logo artwork, watched Ed's video and now here you are." She continued to glare at him as he took out a writing pad.

"Sounds fun. That's exactly why I'm here, isn't it? This whole office is overworked and we need to take care of that as our first priority. I'll need an office to work from, preferably close to yours, please." She groaned inwardly as his words sank in. "I have a vast array of reports and paperwork that Ed has provided me and I've been studying those most of the night.

What I don't have is first hand accounts of what is happening here. What safeguards failed and led to the current situation. I want to put your mind at rest Emily. I'm not here for a shake-up. I'm here to help you put the wheels back on this bus and make sure it gets going smoothly again. Preferably with all of the current passengers."

"Nice analogy. I'd suggest you don't let the other staff hear you calling them passengers. Especially those ones I'll have to shoo out of the office at nine o'clock tonight."

"I didn't mean they were cruising along." He scribbled words on his page and frowned at his pen. "Are you going to be this defensive the whole time I'm here? Three months is a long time to hate me every day."

"Three months? You're here for three months?"

"Yep. Enough time to get a full complement of staff into place and then analyse what can be improved." He looked up at her stricken face. "It's not going to be a problem is it?" His lips twitched, like he wanted to grin at her again, but didn't dare.

Damn right, you shouldn't grin at me. I badly want to kill you right now.

The silence stretched between them as she considered her answer.

Was there going to be a problem? Could she see him every day at work for three months and not end up dreading coming in every day? Would he stay out of her way or would he be underfoot asking questions about everything she and the other staff did? She was the human resources manager for the company, surely that meant he wouldn't be required to supervise her as she hired new staff. If he could take some of the load off her shoulders she could get back to what she was meant to be doing.

"There'll be no problem Cooper as long as we remain businesslike at all times. I don't expect a whisper of our history to get to anyone in this office. Is that understood?"

"Sure. Of course I'd never mention it."

"Right. I'll let Ed know what we've talked about and we'll go from there. Come with me—there's an office across the hall that's empty." She swept past him, not checking to see if he followed. She flicked the light on and removed some boxes stacked on the table. "This office was empty long before we fired our entire management team. When we rehire, you won't have to move out."

"Great. I'll get settled and then can you and I go over the staff list please? I want to know who is who and how you think they're performing."

"Oh great. Like they're not wary of me enough already. Let's make the first task to have them hating you, too."

He laughed, a sound she hadn't expected. Her manner was cold toward him and he wasn't reacting to it at all. His ready smile hadn't faltered since he'd arrived and she wondered what it would take to get him ruffled.

Scratch that. I do not wonder anything about Cooper Jackson. Not ever.

~

*T*he bang of her office door across the hall telegraphed everything to him it was supposed to. She was pissed to be stuck working with him and nothing he could do would change that.

That's where she was wrong, though. Three months working closely with him was guaranteed to remind her of the fun they'd had together. Maybe it had only been for a few weeks, but he'd thought they'd had a good thing going. He'd tied up any casual loose ends he had lying around and was happy he'd finally found someone to get serious with.

Two weeks later she'd stopped returning his calls.

No warning. Just silence. He'd worried something had happened to her, until he'd seen her having lunch with some friends. That's when it dawned on him she was ignoring him on purpose. To test his theory he sent her a text and watched carefully as she picked up her phone, read the message, then shook the phone above her head like she was shaking pancake mixture. When she'd thrown it back into her bag without replying he'd known they were done.

He just didn't know why.

Enter Ed Simpson all these months later. His enquiry to see if Cooper was available for a corporate rescue had been mildly interesting. After he'd signed on and had been provided with all the company reports he'd been ecstatic to discover Emily Pennington listed on the payroll as the human resources manager. He'd spent an hour over breakfast trying to work out a plan to get her to go out with him again. He'd assured Ed nothing like that would happen, though, so he'd have to settle for softening her up during his time here. Three months working with her would give him a chance to work out what he'd done to upset her. From the calculated smirk he'd seen on her face, she thought she could palm him off on the other staff, but he'd work out a plan to spend most of his time with her, chipping away at her resolve.

In three months, if he played this right, she'd be unable to resist him.

CHAPTER 2

"*A*lright Em, spill. What's so important that we had to convene a special lunch on a workday? You know we are weekend friends, right?" Jordan rolled her eyes at Emily as the two other women seated at the table laughed.

"Yeah Emily," Andrea chimed in, "don't you know we are giving up dry biscuits and cottage cheese at our desks to eat pizza with you? It better be worth it."

"Oh it's worth it, though I wonder why I keep you lot around!"

"Relax," Shelly squeezed her hand. "They're just teasing. Tell us what's happened."

"You remember Cooper who I dated last year for a little while?"

"I remember him. He came with us to that awful

baseball game." Jordan took a sip of her drink, waiting for Emily to share her news.

"That's him. Well, he showed up yesterday at my work."

"Is he stalking you?"

"That could be romantic."

She held up her hands as her friends teased her. "You guys! This is serious." They quieted down and she continued. "He's been sent by my boss to help me replace all the staff we've lost recently. He's being paid a tonne of money to consult on our rescue mission."

"And you're unhappy about it?"

"Yes, I'm unhappy! I broke off all contact with him and now I have to spend a chunk of each day sitting across a boardroom table from him. What am I going to do?"

"Enjoy the view, I'd say. I seem to recall he's a tall, gorgeous surfer dude. You could have worse things to stare at all day." Shelly giggled and the others joined in.

"I don't have time to gaze at him, regardless of whether I want to or not. I'm so busy! I only had time to be here today because he insisted I take an hour for lunch and said he'd hold the fort."

"Didn't he arrive yesterday? How can he cover for you after only one day?"

"Thank you, Jordan, my point exactly! Who does

he think he is, sending me to lunch? I have tonnes to do and he sends me out to eat salad and chat to my girlfriends. The hide of that man." She drank her water and motioned to the waiter to bring her a refill. "How am I going to get rid of him?" Her three friends stared at her in silence. Shelly was obviously trying not to laugh judging from the strange choking noise she kept making and the other two looked back at her, confused. "What?"

"Why did you break up with Cooper?"

"Yes, I seem to recall you said it didn't work out, but you didn't say much else."

"I caught him on the phone with someone else."

"Oooh, really? Why didn't you tell us?"

"I was upset at the time and I didn't want to talk about it. Shelly was getting married, Jordan was pretending she didn't love Luke." She grinned as her friend rolled her eyes. "Oh stop it Jordan, all of us could see it, except you. Anyway, there was never a right time and I just got on with things. We'd only been out a few times so I chalked it up to him being the wrong guy."

"So who was he talking to?"

"I don't know but it was a woman. He kept telling her she was beautiful and that she knew he loved her and he'd be with her soon. His actual words before I walked into the room were 'maybe in a few weeks we can get back together.'"

"Wow. Why didn't you ask him about it?"

"I wanted to, but I didn't want to seem clingy."

"It could have been grandma."

"His sister."

"Come on you guys," Shelly reined them in. "It sounds like it totally could have been another woman. That's what you thought wasn't it, Em?"

"I didn't know what to think. I thought he might tell me about it but when I walked into the room he hastily said goodbye and hung up. He actually smiled at me and said he was on a work call!"

"Oh crap! Maybe we should be drinking wine for this conversation." Jordan signalled to the waiter but Emily turned and shook her head at him.

"No, I can't go back to the office if I've been drinking. Water will have to do." She clinked glasses with Jordan and downed her water as if it were straight alcohol. "At first I planned to ask him about it, but then the next day he started getting all these texts to his phone. He answered them all through lunch but never once said what he was doing. On the way home I finally asked him and he dismissed it as work again. I wasn't convinced so I took a giant step back and didn't reply to his calls for a bit. A few days stretched into weeks and then it felt too awkward and I just let it go. I felt guilty not to be honest with him but he was already hiding whatever it was from me. It was better to move on. If it was his grandma, he'd have said so, wouldn't he?"

They sat in silence for a few moments until Andrea finally spoke up. "I think he would have told you if it was something innocent. The fact he didn't means it was something he didn't want you to know about. After what you heard, I agree it sounds like another woman."

"Well, that should make you feel better. You made the right decision to not see him again."

"But now she has one problem with the 'not seeing him again plan'." Jordan waved her hands around to make air quotes.

Emily nodded. "He's sitting in the office across from mine for the next three months."

$\sim$

*L*unch with the girls didn't sort out Emily's dilemma but she did feel better now she had unloaded the story to them. She'd left out one vital part, though. The part where she'd been heartbroken to end it nine months ago. The part where she'd even thought Cooper had seemed like he might be 'the one'. Until she'd overheard that phone call, there'd been a nervous flutter in her stomach every time she saw him. The couple of times he'd kissed her goodbye her toes had curled up right inside her shoes. The memory of his hands in her hair and his fingers skimming her back were vivid, even now. Every second of their short weeks together was imprinted on her brain.

Too bad he hadn't been honest with her about whoever else he was seeing. She'd been ready to get serious with him but he'd messed it up. Now she had to endure twelve weeks of wondering what could have been.

CHAPTER 3

"Okay, spread these out over the table and let's make some hard decisions." Cooper moved the pages so they were evenly spaced and then picked up a whiteboard market. "I wanted to do this yesterday but better late than never. First, we need a list of all the positions we're missing. Hit me with your thoughts."

"You saw what happened yesterday. There's so much happening here I can barely get anything done. But it's day two and you're right into it. Maybe we should fire everyone and start from scratch."

"Do you think that's what needs to happen?" he turned and looked at her, like she might be serious.

"Of course not! God, you're frustrating." She glared at the list in front of her before looking up at him again. "Let's start with who we removed. We have no operations manager, no accounts manager

17

and no sales manager. If we employ each of those people they could choose their own teams."

"That's possible, but we don't have time to muck around. I want to employ everyone we need—the new managers can work with whatever staff we give them. If we give the managers time to get settled and they do their own hiring, months will pass before everyone is on board. Can't happen." He wrote the positions on the board as she watched the muscles ripple across his back inside his business shirt.

Damn him. Why can't he keep his jacket on?

"Who else?"

She got up and turned the air conditioning down two notches before she replied, "Five staff left us. Two sales people, one accounts person, one from the warehouse and one HR assistant." She flicked through the pages in her hand. "We had also planned to put on five new staff before everything went to shit."

A knock sounded on the door and Sasha stuck her head in. "I'm sorry to interrupt but the air conditioning contractor is here and he needs a permit written to access the roof."

"Can't someone else do it?" Cooper was quick to question Sasha but she shook her head as Emily stood up.

"It's fine Sasha, I'll be down in a second." She turned back to Cooper, "Get used to these interruptions. They go on all day every day from sun up to sun down and sometimes beyond."

"There's no one else to write a permit?"

"Company policy states only senior managers write working at height permits. We had four people authorised to do it. Now there's only me. I'll be back as soon as I can."

Thirty minutes later she slipped back into her seat. "Right, we were talking about the five positions we had already been short before the exodus."

"We were. What were those positions?"

He again scribbled on the board as she spoke. "Another sales person, one person in accounts, one in customer service, a warehouse assistant and another in purchasing."

"How the hell have you been managing when you're missing ten staff across all departments?"

"You already know the answer to that. We're working longer hours, everybody has taken on extra tasks and some things are slipping through the cracks."

"Hmmm. You're doing extraordinarily well," he mused as he gazed at the whiteboard.

Is he complimenting me? What's with this guy?

He soon reverted to expectations as he turned to her and said, "You lost an assistant? Why?" His tone was accusing, implying her staff weren't loyal to her.

"My assistant happened to be married to the sales

manager, if you must know. When we removed him, she quit on the spot."

"Oh. That must have been uncomfortable."

"It was an awful time. Some days I wanted to stay in bed and quit myself. We can't go on much longer like this. There are whispers that a few more people might leave if the workload isn't reduced soon. Our people are hard workers—they don't like to feel it is impossible to reach their goals."

"That's why I'm here!" he turned his surfer smile on her and she gave him a tiny smile in return as he slipped into one of the empty seats. "I see your frosty demeanour is slipping. I told you taking a lunch break would make you feel better."

"Don't flatter yourself Cooper. Though I did enjoy catching up with the girls, so thank you for that. It's been weeks since I've had the time to see them."

The phone on the desk rang and Emily picked it up, then rolled her eyes and sighed, "Send her to the conference room please. I can sign those while we're in this meeting."

Cooper frowned. "My first priority has to be getting new staff in here so we can start training them and take some of that workload off you and the others. How soon can you start advertising these positions?"

"We have standard ads already written for the ten positions. I can get my assistant to place them today and tomorrow. The management ones will take a little more work since we haven't needed to fill those roles in a while."

Another knock on the door and a woman appeared with a stack of papers. "Here's the cheques for signing, and purchasing added a pile of orders that need authorising too. Just call when they're done and I'll come and get them if you like. Oh, this one is urgent, if you could sign it now I'll take it with me." She paused as Emily checked the paperwork and signed the cheque. "Cory was looking for you, too."

"Great. Tell Cory I'll call him when I'm out of this meeting." The door closed and she returned her eyes to Cooper.

"This is bloody insane," he said and she shrugged.

"It is what it is."

"Well, we're going to fix it. Get the job ads out as soon as you can. Put everything else aside until they're up. Can we meet back here at four o'clock to go over the current staff? I want to assess each one."

She stood and gathered the papers but he put his hand on hers, "Leave them. I want to look through them." She snatched her hand away and moved toward the door. "Oh, and Emily?"

"Yes?" she sighed and closed her eyes before turning her head slightly in his direction.

"We'll be here late tonight. Can you organise us some chinese or something?"

Jesus Christ, on top of everything else, now I'm organising his dinner?

~

*A*nnoying Emily was amusing Cooper a little too much and he needed to stop. Acting in a professional manner was a trait he took particular pride in, but being around her had triggered an immediate reaction. He'd promised Ed there was nothing between them and that *had* been the truth two days ago when they'd discussed it. Seeing her again had thrown him, though. He thought he was over her; had long forgotten that she rejected him and moved on, with no explanation. All it took was a waft of her perfume and he was lost again.

Now he needed to find a way for them to spend a lot of time together—a way for him to convince her to give him a second chance. How was he going to do that when every chance she got, she scurried out of the conference room to pass on jobs to her assistant, or deal with something on the site? Even a closed-door meeting was interrupted multiple times taking her attention away. He needed a plan to keep her close and her attention on him.

~

*A*t four o'clock Emily dutifully appeared at the conference room door. She noted with satisfaction that Cooper had put his jacket on as the room cooled. Hiding her smirk, she dumped the pile of files she was carrying on the edge of the table.

His head shot up. "What are those?"

"Personnel files. There's more." She returned with another pile, her computer perched on the top, and placed them beside the first. "Be aware the sight of me with all of these has set tongues wagging." She flopped into the nearest chair and opened her laptop.

"You don't have electronic versions?"

"We do but they're saved in separate files all over the shared drive. I don't have time to flick between them so I brought the actual files." She closed the lid of her laptop and leaned toward him. "I need to ask you something and I want you to tell me the truth, please." He inclined his head and watched as she gathered herself. "You're not planning to close us down, are you? Your intention is genuinely to get us back on our feet without any redundancies?"

"Of course it is. Why would you think different?"

"I don't, but several people have asked today if they were going to lose their jobs. I wanted to make sure I wasn't lying when I told them their jobs were safe."

"You weren't lying. Their jobs are safe as long as we decide their roles are necessary to the smooth running of this place. I don't have instructions to close you down, only to ensure things quickly get back to normal." He raised his eyebrows. "Does that make you feel better?"

"It does. How do I know I can trust you, though?"

"I've given you no reason not to."

She stared at him, recalling the overheard phone call and the secretive text messages all those months ago. Finally, she answered, "I guess not."

"What does that mean?"

"Nothing. Just that I have no way of knowing about your level of honesty. I'll have to take your word for it."

"I guess so." He ground the words out between clenched teeth.

A vein tapped in his head and she could see she'd annoyed him.

Good. It's about time someone besides me was annoyed in this room.

"Shall we start?" she opened her laptop again, ignoring him standing over her and glaring. "Who do you want first?"

"Start with the top file. I have the organisation chart here - I'll tick off each one as we go through. By the way, I emailed Ed and I'm now authorised to sign cheques and purchase orders. Next time they need doing, direct them to me."

"What? Just like that he gave you signing authority?"

"He did. You cannot continue like this, being interrupted every minute of the day. The business needs you. So I took care of it."

Ed must really trust you to give you that kind of

control. If only he knew you were capable of lying, like anyone.

"Will he—"

"An email is being drafted to all staff as we speak. By the morning they'll all know. I have an appointment with the bank to be added to the signatory list."

She stared at him for a microsecond, considering every argument why this was a bad idea. Then she thought of the long nights at work and how she hadn't left the office before nine o'clock over the last few months, and she pinched her lips together.

Let him sign whatever he wants if it means I get some time back.

They settled down to work and went through each staff member in the first pile of folders, categorising their role and making lists of the tasks that each person did. They also discussed which new staff member each person would be able to help train as the positions were filled. With so many new employees about to join the company they'd need help to on-board each one.

The last thing Cooper wanted was Emily training ten new staff and overseeing their every move. He'd just freed up some of her time; filling it again with low-level tasks that didn't include him was not part of his master plan.

"Okay, so here's a tough one." Emily slid the file across the desk to him. "Heather has worked here for fourteen years. She has two small children and has an impeccable record. The problem is, her technology skills aren't up to scratch. Somehow she has bumbled through but she does a lot of things manually, when they could be electronic. She has paper files because she doesn't trust 'that computer' as she calls it."

"Hmm… that can't be a good use of her time."

"No, but I wouldn't want to see her go. It would be mighty unfair of us to finish her up. She's been an enormous help over the last few months too, always taking on extra work. A little bird told me she did most of the filing for the whole building last month. That can't have been fun."

"Okay, so we train her better. Or send her somewhere for training."

"Good. That's what I hoped you'd say."

"I'm glad. I wouldn't want you to think I was an ogre or anything." His words resulted in an immediate eye roll and she opened the next folder.

At seven o'clock her phone chimed and she glanced at the screen. "That's dinner. I'll be back."

"Do you need me to come too?"

Emily snickered. "I'm a big girl and I certainly don't need an escort to the door. Besides, there are still at least ten people hard at work in the office. I think my virtue will remain intact." She swept out of the room leaving his reply dead on his lips.

When she returned she carried a bag of food, cutlery and two plates. She laid them on the table and slid two cans of drink across the table. He reached for his and looked up at her as he opened the can. "Hey Passiona, you remembered."

"It was that or Coke."

"Yes, but you remembered that Passiona is my favourite, didn't you?"

"Shut up and eat your food."

They opened the containers and shared out the contents. While they ate Sasha called up to say goodbye and the office gradually quieted down.

"Emily?"

"Mmm…?"

"Before, when I offered to come down with you. I meant did you want me to pay for dinner. I wasn't implying that you weren't capable of taking care of yourself."

She chewed and watched him, feeling sick inside. Here she was telling herself how professional she was, and suddenly she was putting words in his mouth and trying her best to put him in his place. She didn't normally behave like this and it needed to stop. They needed to call a truce if they were going to make this work. The last thing she needed was to lose her job because she'd reacted badly to him being in the office. "I'm sorry Cooper. I'm on edge, that's all. It's been a tough few months, the staff all have trust issues and your arrival hasn't helped. I didn't think I'd ever see you again, and I certainly didn't expect you to show up at my workplace. Give me some time and I'll get it together. Things are moving fast and I just need to adjust."

"Do you need some time off?"

She frowned at him and anger flared in her chest. "No, I do not need time off. See, that's what irritates me. Stop being so accommodating. I have a job to do —let me do it."

"Okay, okay." He dropped his fork and raised his hands. "No more being nice to you. Got it."

CHAPTER 4

*S*everal days later the job applications started rolling in. Cooper suggested they go through them together and Emily ground her teeth together at this latest intrusion. This was something she or her assistant would normally do. It wasn't a task that required a consultant who was probably being paid six figures to make improvements.

Since Cooper had arrived, she'd barely been able to shake him. The first two days they'd gone through the current staffing and advertised the vacant positions. He'd insisted she escort him across the site and explain the intricacies of each department. Several times she'd suggested that a staff member from that area should take over but all he'd done was accept their input, and insist she stick around. Her workload had been juggled between her assistant and a casual staff member to free up her time and he seemed quite pleased with his efforts.

If she didn't know better, she would swear he was doing it on purpose.

They planned to spend the afternoon looking at the audit trails of the accounting department and once again, he'd insisted she be included as well as the one remaining staff member from accounts. Whatever he was up to, she was determined to say nothing and remain professional at all times. In a few months he'd be gone.

She entered the conference room and watched as he hastily switched his phone off and slipped it into his pocket.

Just like old times.

"How many applications do we have?"

"Tonnes. We've split them up by role but there's still a lot to sift through. Plenty will be completely unsuitable but you said you wanted to see all of them so here they are. Jenny printed all the online applications and she's split them into the different positions. What do you want first?"

"First I want the ones for the HR assistant. I want your staff sorted out so you can apply yourself to more appropriate tasks. Jenny seems like she's a great help but I can see she's here late each night, too."

"I don't need your favouritism. Mine can wait."

He pulled the pile she indicated toward him. "NO, they can't. It's not favouritism, it's common sense.

You're running this place right now. You don't need to be doing your own filing or replying to job applications because you only have one assistant."

"Let's look at the operations manager roles then. Wouldn't it make sense to get one of those first?"

"No. Trust me, okay? Applicants for that role are far more likely to be already in jobs and able to sit tight. Plus, they apply for fewer roles because there are fewer that suit them. The ones for admin roles are often about to leave their job or have already left. They apply for hundreds of positions and they can be snapped up before you get back to them."

"Are you explaining my job to me? Really?"

"I'm not telling you how to suck eggs, I'm just saying that I have a specific set of priorities. If you weren't here and handling everything so well I'd be looking for an operations manager at the first opportunity. But I do have you, and that gives us some leeway. Make sense?"

"Maybe. The jury is still out. If you turn out to be correct on this I will admit to seeing a different perspective."

He grinned and gave a triumphant bow. "Great. Let's see what we've got shall we? I want us both to go through the whole lot. You check my discard pile and I'll check yours and we'll discuss."

"No, that's a waste of time - let's go through each one together."

He waved his arm in front of him. "If that's what

you want, let's do it. We have accounting coming at one so I ordered us some lunch."

"Did you just?"

"Yep. Sasha will bring it at twelve."

She scowled at him and vowed to bring her lunch tomorrow. The less time she spent alone with Cooper, the better.

They set about going through the applications, separating the resumes into yes and no piles, several times arguing over a candidate's suitability. The time quickly slipped by and when Sasha arrived with a chicken salad for Emily and a burger for Cooper, Emily scowled all over again.

Bastard. Being considerate and ordering me a healthy lunch.

They ate in silence, Cooper sipping his Passiona and grinning at her while she rolled her eyes. After lunch they quickly finished the sorting and Emily passed the piles to Jenny so she could organise the appointments. When she returned to the conference room Cooper had another surprise in store for her.

"Sorry, I forgot to say I wanted the interviews planned a certain way."

"Oh really. You're a total control freak, aren't you? I never noticed that about you until now. What extra demands do you have?"

"Emily, you're so mean to me!" he laughed, not taking offence at her words. "It's easy stuff, don't get all twisted up at me. Just get Jenny to book no more than three interviews each day. I want you to still have time to do other tasks without staying here until midnight. Think about it. If we interview 3 people for each position that's 30 interviews. That's hours and hours out of our day. So we limit it to three each day and don't overwhelm ourselves. As we fill the roles we'll employ them and get them started. I don't know about you but I can't sit in interviews for eight hours a day."

"Well, you don't have to sit through them, so it shouldn't be an issue."

"Oh, did I forget to tell you? I'll be interviewing with you."

She stared at him, stunned. "What? Ed said I had full control to hire."

"And you do. We won't employ anyone you're not convinced is the best person for the job. You always have more than one interviewer, right?"

"Yes." Her mind whirled as she tried to think of a reason someone else should stand in for him.

"Great. Let's not cut into anyone else's day. I'm the only one around here who doesn't have a million paper transactions to process as part of their job. I'll accompany you until we've chosen everyone we need."

She looked down at her feet, wishing she'd thought of something to deter him.

Fuck!

~

The accounting audit took more than three hours and by the end of it Emily never wanted to see another print out of figures again. She'd explained the process they used to make sure every order was authorised by a manager as well as every outgoing payment. Anyone could raise a purchase order as long as his or her manager signed it off. The orders didn't have to go through purchasing, they could be entered directly into the purchasing system and given to a supplier.

"So that's one place we could tighten up to prevent a repeat of what's happened." Cooper was making notes on the whiteboard again. His jacket was on the back of his chair and Emily made a note to check the temperature of every room they worked in from now on. He turned and looked at their last remaining accounts person, Beth. "What suggestions do you have?"

"I think it could be wise to impose a dollar limit. Managers at a certain level can sign up to a certain amount, say two thousand or three thousand dollars. Above that, the order would have to be signed by someone higher up. Also, I think all purchasing should be moved back to the purchasing department. It's spread out everywhere at the moment, I suspect because it saves employing another person."

"One more staff member would have been a lot

cheaper than what the company is facing now," Cooper said and Emily nodded her agreement.

"I think we need some kind of sign off on big sales contracts, too. Maybe even at the quote stage, though that could be over the top."

Beth spoke again, "Any contracts that have any kind of refund or kickback should be signed by a higher manager." She looked at them both. "You know none of this would have stopped what happened? With the three of them working together they would have got around these measures."

"You're right. But we have to remember that we employ people expecting that they'll do their job and not rip the company off. What we need to do is put the checks in place to deter them from thinking it's a good idea in the first place. When we know that people will be checking our processes and making sure paperwork is signed off, there's less chance of temptation or taking a risk with our livelihoods." He stood back and read the notes on the board. "I think this is a great start. I'll get this typed up and if you could both give it a quick glance and check it's what we talked about, I'll forward it to Ed and we'll start implementing."

He turned to Beth, "How are you coping with your workload?"

"There are a lot of tasks that I'm not getting to. I haven't done any filing for a month."

Stop talking. Don't say it!

"I'd be a lot worse off if Emily didn't take the left over invoices home each weekend and enter them for me. It's helped me stay on track and as yet we haven't had any suppliers upset with late payment."

Cooper turned to look at Emily who kept staring at her page. "Is there any pie you don't have your finger in Ms Pennington?"

She smirked and kept looking down as Beth looked between the two of them. "Sorry, did I say something wrong?"

"No Beth." Emily finally looked at her. "Cooper thinks I do too much. I've tried to explain I'm taking up the slack where I can to make sure that all of you guys can manage your workload and you don't decide to throw in the towel. He doesn't approve."

"Well, I approve. Don't forget Cooper, we're all taking work home, too."

"That's going to stop soon, I promise. The next roles we're filling are your two missing co-worker spots. It will be hectic for a while as we get them trained, but at least you'll be able to get all your paperwork up to date quickly. Anyone can file invoices and answer the phone, even on their first day."

She looked up at him with a grateful expression, and Emily felt an unfamiliar surge in the pit of her stomach.

Jealousy.

It can't be jealousy. I'm not jealous of him taking all the credit, I just want the work done.

You're jealous of the way she's looking at him.

No. No, I'm not.

Yes. Yes, you are.

CHAPTER 5

"*E*mily?" Sasha stuck her head in the door. "We have a little problem."

"Oh God, what now? I haven't had a moment of peace since I got here this morning!"

"Well, Lacey Waters is here for her interview. She's a little early because she's brought something with her that she needs me to look after while you interview her."

"What kind of something?"

"A *baby* kind of something!"

"What? She brought her baby to a job interview?"

"Yep. She said that her sitter never showed up and she'd rather bring her kid, and be embarrassed, than miss the interview."

"Well, that's a new one. Are you able to watch the baby?"

"Of course. I wanted to check with you first, though. She looked like she might cry if I said no."

"Okay, look, it's really no issue, so if you're happy to do it, let's just press on. I'll come down soon, just let me make sure Cooper is ready." She got up and crossed the hall to his office. "Nearly ready?"

"Sure.

"Our applicant brought her baby along. You know, for something different."

"Her baby?" Cooper looked blankly at her. "Who brings a baby to a job interview?"

"Lacey Waters, apparently. Her sitter fell through. It's no drama, Sasha is going to watch the baby. I wanted to give you a heads up before you meet her."

"Before I meet the baby?" he grinned and rolled his eyes.

"Man, you're annoying."

~

*L*acey turned out to be a great girl that they both felt an instant connection with. She was friendly, thoughtful in her answers, had great qualifications and she won them both over as soon as she was seated at the table.

"I know there's an elephant in the room so let's get it out of the way first. I know legally you can't ask about my family situation but I want to be clear about it. I had to bring my daughter along today because

I'm changing day care centres and I had a week where she didn't have a placement. I organised a babysitter for this morning but she never showed up."

"It's okay, you don't need to explain any of that."

"I know, but I wanted to reassure you that childcare wasn't an issue in any other week of my life, except this one. I'm available for full time work and I only have the one child.

"It's great of you to clear that up and I appreciate it." Emily said. "It takes bravery to bring your child along when you're not sure what kind of reaction a company will have."

"You're telling me. I wanted to cry all the way here but two of us howling in the car would have been ridiculous!"

∾

*C*ooper and Emily agreed to complete a score sheet and make their decisions about the applicants right after each interview. They sat at Cooper's desk and rehashed Lacey's answers.

"I liked that she didn't let her child deter her and that she faced it head on with us at the very start. That girl has balls."

"She does, but what about work-wise. She'll be your assistant, will it be a problem if she needs time off work for a sick kid or to leave early to do evening pickup."

"I'm surprised at you Cooper." Emily frowned at him before looking back at her notes. "We should be looking at whether she's a good fit for the role, not what her personal situation is."

He sat back in his chair and put down his pen. "You're surprised at me? I continue to be amazed by you. She opened the door for us to consider this as part of her application and you still want to ignore it?"

"I don't *want* to ignore it. It's the law." She frowned at him and continued reading Lacey's resume. "She's totally qualified, is friendly and businesslike, plus she's not afraid to make the hard decisions. I'd say she's a definite yes if no one comes along to outshine her."

"Well, she'll be working for you, you're the best judge. Regardless of the kid thing, I approve."

❧

*B*ack in her office she faced the long list of emails she'd been ignoring all morning. Before she could even click on the first one, two bodies appeared in her doorway. "Emily, the server is down and you're the only one with the security code for IT."

She sighed as she got up from her desk. "I'm on it." She addressed the technician. "How long will it take to fix?"

"It depends what it is but we're hoping it's just a simple server reset."

"I hope so too. Our system cannot be down for too long."

"I understand, I'll have it running as soon as I can."

On the way back from granting them access, two people trailed after her in the hallway. "Emily, I need these cheques signed."

She glanced back and quickly delegated with a smile. "You can take those to Cooper. He has signing authority now." She continued toward her office, pleased to have one less task to complete.

"Emily I need the monthly reports so I can close out the month." She sighed as she sat back at her desk.

Baby steps. In a few weeks there'll be someone new to complete those reports.

"Sorry, I'm going to have to do them at home tonight. You'll have them first thing in the morning. Would you mind chasing Jenny to pull out all the procedures that have been written around these reports? It's one of the first tasks I want to assign to a new person so you won't have this delay again."

"Will do. Sorry to nag." Fiona left with an apologetic smile.

Cooper stuck his head in her door next. "Hey, aren't we meant to have an interview at two o'clock? It's quarter past."

"I know. No sign of her, Jenny says. She's tried calling but there's no answer. I think we have our first no show."

"Crap."

Emily laughed. "Yes, that about sums it up. Be prepared for more. We have a long list of people coming and several are bound to change their minds or get a job before we get to interview them, someone recently informed me." The words dripped sweetly from her lips and he narrowed his eyes at her.

"Have you had lunch?" His abrupt change of direction startled her.

"Not yet."

"Did you bring something with you?"

"Yes, I brought a salad. Why all the questions?"

He stepped into the room and shut the door behind him. "Get your bag, I'll take you to lunch."

"No, really I'm fine."

"You're not fine. You're grumpy and overworked. Let's get a quick bite to eat together so we're feeling refreshed when we do the next interview."

"Why can't you just leave me alone?" She sighed and shook her head as his surfer smile appeared. He turned that smile on when he was sure no one could resist him. More often than not she was the target.

"It's not in my job description to leave you alone. Come on, no arguing." He held out his hand and she grumbled as she grabbed her bag. He opened the door and she avoided his hand, stepping past him and striding down the hall.

He insisted on taking his car and he made small talk as he drove to the corner cafe. She ignored most of what he said and answered with a short grunt here and there.

Get lunch over with and get back to the office.

Cooper had other thoughts, though. While she was thinking of the work piling up while she was gone, he was determined to get her talking and they stayed at lunch a lot longer than she would have liked.

She told him all the sordid details surrounding the removal of the three top executives at Simpsons, including the moment when she knew she would have to contact Ed. "It was awful. I never wanted to be the one to tell him, but I had no choice."

"That's a tough call, especially if you had been wrong."

"Don't I know it? In the end I decided I'd rather be able to look at myself in the mirror, than protect my job if I'd made a mistake. I knew I wasn't wrong, though. The evidence was right there in black and white."

"Ed says they will likely have to go to court and even more likely there will be a hefty fine attached to the outcome."

"He told me they plan to fall on their sword and admit to everything. After all, the moment they became aware of the damage done, they terminated the staff involved right away. Regardless of the disadvantage it put the business into."

"I like Ed."

"Me too. How long have you known him?"

"About eight years. We worked together at a previous firm when his dad sent him out to get business experience away from the family-owned companies. I consulted for him about three years ago and we've kept in touch. Just between you and me, he told me that he would have called me sooner but you were doing such a good job of managing that they got lazy."

"That's nice. What else was I meant to do, though? Suddenly everyone was gone and I was the most senior person. So I just organised for everyone to come to me and took care of things as they cropped up. It didn't win me any friends. I'm sure they think I'm a control freak who succeeded in getting rid of my competition so I could take over."

"It's not like that. I've chatted to a few people and they don't think that."

"Speaking of work," she inclined her head and looked at her watch, "we need to get back."

"You're right." He glanced at his watch. "The next poor victim will be arriving in forty five minutes.

~

*E*mily was quietly confident about the next applicant. Her resume was impeccable and she'd listed a long and varied experience in human resources. When she arrived and Sasha announced her, she seemed like she'd be the perfect fit.

"Kerrie Andrews to see you."

They completed the usual pleasantries and sped through the questions. She seemed knowledgeable about all the right things and Emily was convinced they'd found their first person. Just as Cooper offered Kerrie a quick tour of the office, a mobile phone started ringing.

Kerrie's eyes widened and guilt swept over her face. "Sorry, that's me."

"It's totally fine." Cooper said and watched as she reached down to silence the ring tone.

She didn't silence the tone, though. Instead she picked up the phone, answered it and put it to her ear. "Hi Athena." She said brightly as Emily and Cooper exchanged a glance. "Oh, really? I can't believe that! Why would he say that to you?" She raised a finger at them and bobbed her head from side to side and pushed out of her chair. She moved to the door but didn't leave the room while she continued her conversation. "No way! What did you say to her?" A pause. "Well, that's what she gets for being a total cow." Another pause. "This is all too much. You make sure you put her in her place. Listen, I have to go because I'm in the middle of an interview, but I'll call you the minute I get out, okay? Okay, bye!" She turned back, retook her seat and slipped her phone in her bag. "Sorry about that. So we're going to take a tour of the office and you'll show me where I'll be sitting, yes?"

Before either of them could open their mouths the fire alarm sounded.

"Can you believe this?" Cooper asked Emily. "Is this a test?"

"No, that's the real one. Can you take Kerrie out, I have duties as the chief warden."

"Of course you do." Cooper shook his head as he led the way out of the office. "I'm sorry Kerrie, but you'll have to stay until this is all over now. Standard fire drill procedure."

"No problem. I have nowhere to be. I'll call Athena back to pass the time. My friend is Athena Kelly, have you heard of her?"

"I can't say I have."

"She's an up and coming singer. Any time now she's going to be famous. She says she'll invite me along to her first big concert. How exciting is that?"

Fighting the urge to roll his eyes like he'd watched Emily do so many times since he'd arrived, Cooper delivered her into the safekeeping of Sasha when they reached the roll call area in the car park. He watched as wardens for each area completed their roll call and spoke into walkie-talkies they each carried. A fire truck arrived and men in yellow coats piled out and entered the building. He saw Emily waiting at the entrance to greet them and escort them inside. For the next thirty minutes everyone chatted in the carpark. Cooper made small talk with some of the staff he'd already met and watched as Kerrie talked animatedly on her mobile the entire time.

Eventually they were given the all clear to return to the building and Emily announced to the assembled group that a faulty switch had caused the alarm to sound. Cooper quickly stopped Kerrie from coming back inside as people milled around them. "In light of the fire alarm business how about we save the tour for another time. We'll call and let you know if you've been successful, okay?"

"Oh, okay. I thought it was going pretty well," she frowned, oblivious to what could have caused the change. Then she brightened up, "Will you call me?"

"No. It definitely won't be me."

"Damn. That would have been something to look forward to."

Stunned into silence, Cooper was left with no words as he turned and walked away.

"*D*id you get rid of her?" Emily asked before he could get through her doorway.

"I did. Great minds think alike. She seemed

genuinely surprised that she wasn't getting the tour." He sat opposite her.

"Wow. That girl has the hide of a rhino. I'm so bummed. I thought she was great right up until her phone rang."

"Well, you could still—"

"No way! I'll get Jenny to call Lacey Waters and send her for a medical. I was happy with her so I'll take my chances. Today has pushed me to the edge."

"I don't have as much experience as you do, but is it normal for job applicants to be so odd?"

Emily laughed and pulled a folder toward her. "I'm afraid it can be. It's not unusual to have people interview well and then they are just awful when they start. Or vice-versa. They're terrified during the interview and miraculously get the job, only to be stellar performers who stay for years and years. It's hit and miss—hence the three and six month probation period we have now as employers."

"What's the worst thing that's ever happened to you when you've been interviewing?" He laced his hands behind his head and she smiled at his casual stance.

"Hmm… let me think. It's not the worst thing, but once we were interviewing a man who was a little scruffy and I was wondering if he was actually homeless. He was otherwise a pretty great applicant and we asked if we could have his forklift licence to get a copy. He reached into his jacket for his wallet and a cockroach ran out!"

"What?"

"I swear to god that happened. Right in front of us! I wanted to give him the job but my boss at the time overruled me. That's something I'll never forget." She flicked through the new pile of applications in the folder. "Ready to go through some more resumes?"

"Do we have to? I feel like we did a crap job last time."

"No, we're doing okay. We interviewed two, had one no-show and we still picked one to employ. Pretty good odds."

"If you say so." He sat up in his chair and pulled it forward so he was on the other side of the desk. "What have you got for me?"

"Well, this is my second favourite." She handed it to him and he frowned.

"Are you sure? This guy doesn't have much experience and he's had three jobs in twelve months."

"Oh his application is awful, but smell it." She grinned as he lifted the pages to his nose.

"Good God, what is that?"

"I have no idea. It smells like he took it to the supermarket before he mailed it and sprayed some cheap deodorant on it."

Cooper sniffed again. "Eww… it's awful."

"Ha! If I wasn't so busy I'd interview him just to

see what kind of man sends in a scented resume with hardly any appropriate job experience."

"You said that was your second favourite, which is top of your list?" She handed him a new stack of papers. "I'm scared to look." He squinted and then opened his eyes to look at the pages before him. "Wow."

"I know."

"That's pretty spectacular."

"Yup. Guy *really* loves his car."

The resume Cooper held had a cardboard cover and on the cover was printed a photo that was obviously taken with a phone. A Commodore Sedan stood proudly in the centre. The photo was slightly blurry and the car was dirty, but a frame had been added around it in some sort of clipart program. "Is he proving he has his own transport?" He was trying not to laugh as he kept gazing at the photo. "Do I even need to look inside?"

"No you do not. Flick it to the reject pile. He has never held an accounting job in all of his thirty-two years. I think the unemployment agency must have insisted he send some more applications out this month and he thought 'maybe I should join an accounts team.'"

"Do you have anyone decent in that pile? I'm about ready to call it a day."

"There are plenty of good ones. If we can agree

on enough of them we can organise appointments for all the other roles if you like."

"You went ahead and advertised everything?"

"Yep. I ignored what you said and advertised the lot." She grinned at him. "You're not the only one who does whatever he wants."

"You're evil."

"Thanks. I'm also impatient to get things moving. You're being careful not to overwork me but I have a bit more capacity yet."

"I don't know how. I know you're taking work home, even though you leave here after everyone else."

She sighed. "Whatever, Cooper. Don't give me a hard time about it. Let's just get these people scheduled."

They spent the next hour sorting resumes. Decisions made, Emily handed the pile to Jenny who set about making appointments, and before they left that night they had a schedule of who they'd be seeing for the next several weeks.

Emily made sure the woman whose resume said she could be contacted at Im_yr_slutbunny69@dickmail.com didn't get an interview.

CHAPTER 6

"*I* ruined a perfectly good interview yesterday, you guys."

"Oh no, Andrea. What happened?"

"The interviewer asked me what I'd do if people were talking on the front desk. It's a job at the council and they have a rule about no chatting out there. You have to go behind the wall if you want to talk, or something. Anyway, she asked if I would report them to a superior and I said of course I wouldn't. I'd just remind them of the rules and ask them to go behind the wall, and that I'd stay out the front to make sure no customers were left unattended."

"That sounds fair."

"The moment the words were out of my mouth I knew I wasn't getting that job. She pursed her lips and made a note on her notepad that she kept hidden from me. Then she said the working hours are eight in the morning until four forty four in the afternoon and I laughed. The shutters actually came down over her eyes as I giggled and I knew I was done!"

"Why such odd hours?"

"Something to do with a rostered day off? Instead of getting an RDO each month you work sixteen minutes less each day. And they're strict about it, you aren't allowed to stay later without permission."

Emily laughed. "That's pretty standard for council. I can't believe you laughed when she said it."

"I couldn't either but I was so surprised. I'm used to staying at work until everything is done for the day. I couldn't bare to be watching the clock for the exact moment I had to down tools."

They passed the bread around the dinner table and their conversation all too quickly turned to Emily.

"So Emily, tell us how things are going with Cooper. Did you give in and date him yet?"

"No! Of course not. He doesn't even want to date me. We've settled into a comfortable working arrangement and soon he'll be out of my hair. Do you know he's insisting on sitting in on every single interview?"

"Uh huh. Of course he is, and he's not interested in you at all. I think you might be confused about that." Shelly and Boyd both laughed as he wrapped his arms around her shoulder. "Boyd was underfoot for weeks before he got brave enough to ask me out."

"It's true Emily. I was besotted—always thinking up ways we could run into each other or 'accidentally' meet." He grinned at Shelly and she kissed him on the cheek.

"Stop you guys! We've been through this. Cooper and I are not going to happen. He had his chance and he blew it. I do have an offer for you though, Andrea." She turned to her friend who was flicking through the menu. "I want you to apply for one of our admin jobs. You didn't find anything yet, did you?"

"The council was my last interview except for a second interview booked for next week at the job that is my number one pick, but besides that I'm still available."

"Okay, perfect. Send me your resume, go to that second interview and if it doesn't work out I want you to interview for a job with us. You'd be perfect and you'd like working there. The people are great!"

"All the people?" Andrea waggled her eyebrows as the rest of the table laughed.

"All except one and he'll be gone soon."

~

"Cooper?"

He looked up and she could have sworn his eyes lingered on her legs a moment too long. "Yes?"

"I've asked my friend Andrea to apply for one of

the admin roles. She's looking for a new job and when I told her we were having some adventures in our own hiring we got to talking about it. If you're impressed by her resume, I'll need to excuse myself from the interview, but I wanted you to know why."

"Uh... okay. When will we have it?"

"She's emailing it today. I already know she'd be great, otherwise I wouldn't have suggested it. We're close friends, though, and it will be immediately apparent to the other staff so it's best I remove myself."

"Fair enough. Sometimes I wonder which one of us is more of a stickler for the rules, you know." He laughed as she frowned and walked back to her office. Even when she closed the door she could hear him chuckling.

Why on earth would he compare us like that?

~

"I'm so sorry, we seem to be missing our other panel member. Could you take a seat and I'll see where she's gone." Cooper indicated the chair in front of him and their newest applicant sat down.

He almost sprinted from the room in search of Emily. He found her writing a work at height permit for an electrician planning work in the roof. He stepped back to wait for her and when she was finished she scolded him. "Why didn't you stay with her? I would have only been a few minutes."

"I have to tell you something first." He grabbed her arm and pulled her down the hallway.

"Why are you whispering?"

"Here." He ducked into an empty office off the corridor and flicked on the lights. He closed the door behind him and Emily could see his face was bright red.

"What's wrong?" Fear clutched at her throat.

What has happened to him to make him look like that?

"I've done a terrible thing."

"Don't keep me in suspense!"

"Well, we're interviewing Cindy Fong, right? I go out there to get her and there's more than one person sitting in reception. I walk over to her and call out her name when I'm standing almost in front of her. Except it's not her."

"I don't understand what you're talking about."

"The Asian woman who I stood in front of, with my hand extended, was not Cindy Fong." He dragged his fingers through his hair and stared at her. "Cindy Fong is not Asian. She's as Caucasian as you or I. I just racially profiled the poor woman that we're about to interview based on her surname!"

Emily leaned against the desk, a giggle desperate to escape her chest. "It's not so bad."

"Oh yes it is. It's bad. Bad, bad, bad, bad, bad! I

have to sit through an interview with her now, knowing that she had to walk across the room and tap me on the shoulder to introduce herself!"

"Oh, wow. You really made sure you couldn't cover that up, didn't you?"

"I apologised several times but I felt awful. She took it well but I'm still worried."

"Come on, then." She patted him on the shoulder as she walked past. "It'll be fine. Let's hope she's great and we can all laugh about this a few years from now."

The interview *was* great and when they compared their score sheets after the meeting, they both agreed that Cindy Fong was a definite yes for an accounting role.

"Thank God." Cooper said. "Lawsuit avoided!"

~

Keryth Belvin positively bounced into the conference room as Sasha grinned and closed the door behind her. Cooper and Emily shook her hand and she settled herself in her chair, still beaming at them.

"It's nice to meet you both!" she enthused. "I'm so excited to be here!"

A tap on her foot told Emily that Cooper thought this girl was odd. She smiled kindly at her and slipped her foot away. Playing footsies with him was not a good way to keep her mind on the interview.

They asked the usual questions and dutifully noted down the answers. Keryth was just as excited toward the end of the interview as she was at the start, and Cooper finally commented on her sunny nature. "Oh, I'm always cheery. Nothing that ever happens is bad enough to make me sad. I always make the best of a bad situation and can find something to laugh about. It helps that I'm convinced you're going to hire me!" she said with an enormous grin.

"You do?" Emily couldn't resist. "Why's that?"

"Did you look at my resume?"

"Umm... of course, but—"

"Well, if you check again you'll see that it's my eighteenth birthday today! I could be off having lunch with my friends or getting ready for my party tonight, but instead I'm here at your job interview." She smiled her sunny smile again and glanced at them both. "That shows I'm dedicated and really want this role, which makes me perfect. I bet no-one else is here on their birthday."

Cooper laughed and it was Emily's turn to kick him under the table. "You're right. No one else has tried to blackmail us by pointing out their date of birth. Very clever of you."

"I just didn't want it to go unnoticed. I want this job and I think I'd be great at it, from what you've explained. Please consider me seriously before you make a decision."

"We definitely will. Thanks for coming in, it really does show dedication." Emily couldn't be mean to her; the girl was just so damn cheerful.

They escorted her out and met back in the conference room to compare score sheets.

"Besides the birthday bribery, what do you think?" Emily asked.

"Well, she'd definitely be pleasant to have around, though she may turn out to be a bit of a chatterbox. She's very young but we are employing a basic accounts person in this one. It's nice to have some variety in the office age-wise. New ideas are always good."

"I agree. Let's short list her."

"We only have one more to interview for accounts don't we? Do you think we've seen enough people?"

"Yes, definitely. I don't believe in continuing to interview when you've found suitable applicants. It's like looking at wedding dresses when you've already bought yours and it's hanging in your cupboard. There'll always be something better."

"Interesting. Okay, she's a yes if the next one isn't better. Good."

"Let's hope whoever we appoint to the accounts manager role, likes chirpy young ladies in their team."

$\curlyvee$

*T*he third job applicant turned out to be the most exciting of all. The conference room had a previous booking so they held it in Cooper's office instead.

Stacy Cook was doing well. She was articulate and gave all the right answers to their questions. She continually wiped her hands across her skirt, showing how nervous she was and when it came time for her to ask questions, her hands visibly shook. "I'm drawing a blank." She stared at them, wide-eyed. "I'm sure there's something clever or insightful I'm meant to ask here but I just can't think of anything. You covered all the details I would normally want to know." She smiled at them both and Emily took pity on her.

"That's okay. There's no rule that says you have to ask questions. If you think of anything after you've gone home, feel free to call me." Emily slid her card across the table. Stacy wiped her hand again before she took the card and dropped it into the handbag she'd placed beside her chair. Cooper thanked her for coming and she stood and shook both their hands.

She took a step to her right and the toe of her shoe caught in the handle of her bag. Suddenly she was flailing through the air and she fell heavily against the side table. As she continued her downward trajectory, she knocked a photo frame from the table and it smashed onto the floor, the glass breaking into several pieces.

"Oh my gosh, I'm so sorry!" she howled, before dropping to her knees.

"It's okay, just leave it." Cooper was quick to take her elbow to help her up. "We can clean that up."

"No, no. I'll do it. I'm so clumsy. So sorry!" She rubbed her hand along the carpet, trying to scoop up the glass. A large piece stuck into her palm and cut through the skin. Emily jumped up as blood spurted from Stacy's hand, some of it dripping on the floor.

"Oh my goodness." Emily pushed a box of tissues across the desk. "Let me go and get a first aid kit." She rushed to the kitchen, leaving Cooper to deal with the bleeding, and now bawling, woman. When she returned Stacy was howling and trying to wipe blood off the shoulder of Cooper's suit. He was saying soothing words to her and managed to finally get her into a chair, where she covered her face and let out huge wracking sobs.

Cooper and Emily stared at each other, both with helpless expressions. They offered her tissues and repeated that it was totally fine. When she finally had herself under control, they took care of her hand and Emily walked her down the stairs and out to her car. She promised to call when they had made their decision. As she stood and watched the car drive away, she cringed as she heard a backfire echo down the street.

That girl has had one difficult day!

Cooper flopped into the chair opposite her desk the moment she was back upstairs. "Have you ever had a day like this?"

"Nothing surprises me any more. But no, today was a one-of-a-kind experience. I'm exhausted."

"Me too. Imagine if we'd booked more than three!"

She pursed her lips. "You don't have to rub it in Cooper. You were right, okay?"

"I'm not trying to rub anything in. I'm just saying *imagine how crap today would have been if more crazies had been scheduled.*" The look on his face made Emily laugh and she relaxed. Something she hadn't done in his presence since he'd arrived last week. "I know you'll say it's inappropriate and that you're not interested, but do you want to get dinner with me? The apartment is boring on my own and I'm tired of eating frozen pizza."

"Damn, I was going to suggest we get a pizza. Oh well." Her lips twitched as she made fun of him. "Maybe I can make an exception and we could get a pub meal?"

"Perfect." Pleasure filled his voice and his face. "I have a few emails to answer then let's get out of here."

"I'll need at least thirty minutes. Plus I'll need to organise someone else to lock up."

"Sounds good. I'll see you when you're ready."

Dinner with Cooper. What the hell am I thinking?

CHAPTER 7

*D*inner with Cooper was a lot more pleasant than Emily would have liked. He'd always been fun and more than one date had ended in them laughing uncontrollably together. Just like old times, they were soon laughing and joking together tonight.

"How's your parrot?"

"He's great. You'll see him tomorrow. I'm having pest control done at my house and they said not to leave him locked inside all day the first day. So I'll bring him to work."

"I noticed the stand in the corner of your office."

"I don't bring him in often and lately I just haven't had time to bother about it. Everyone loves him, though. It makes the office a chatty place whenever he's there."

"How's your crazy friend Jordan doing? Did she ever manage to settle on one guy?"

"First, she's not crazy. You use that word a lot and I suspect it is highly inappropriate. Jordan was just trying a new way to meet the right man. Second, her and Luke are engaged."

"Luke? I met him the night of the toilet-bowl-around-the-neck incident didn't I? They seemed like they were just friends."

"Yes, well, Luke felt a bit stronger than that and Jordan finally realised she felt the same too. It took all year though! He asked her to marry him on New Year's Eve so she almost reached her goal." She popped a mouthful of roast beef into her mouth and chewed. "We're counting it as a win."

"Definitely. So she ditched the toilet bowl guy, what was his name?"

"Richard."

"That's it. He seemed fun."

"Yep, turns out a bit too fun. She wasn't the only one."

"Wow. How could he do that to her? If he was serious he should have finished up with the others."

Oh, this from you!

She paused before she answered. "I guess some people like to keep their options open. One of his options was his wife."

"Wow!"

"Yeah. Jordan said a lot worse things than that."

"Have you ever cheated on someone?"

Have you?

"No, why would you ask me that?"

"No reason. I'd never do that so I wondered."

"You'd never go out with one woman while you were dating another?"

"Of course not."

"Have you ever? Even once?"

"Nope." He sipped his drink and watched as she put her cutlery down. "I don't want to ruin the friendly atmosphere we've got going here by discussing our private life, but when you and I met, I immediately curtailed my activities with anyone else."

Sure you did!

"Really? Why?"

"Because I thought we had something. I thought you felt it too. Turns out I was way off base."

She bit her lip, and considered telling him what she'd overheard and asking him to explain it to her. Nine months had passed, though, and now they were working together. Nothing good could come of making him confess that he *was* seeing someone else back then. Work would be awkward and she still had many weeks of working with him. Best to change the subject.

"You'll need to get your suit dry cleaned."

"Luckily I brought more than one with me for just such an occurrence."

"No one could have predicted today. We didn't even compare our score sheets."

"I left mine on my desk for tomorrow. I thought she was a great candidate but she was so nervous. If that was just interview nerves we can overlook it. If she'll be like that every time there's a problem or a hard decision to make, then she's not a good fit."

"I agree. Let's do the other interviews and then get her back for a second if we need to."

"Good idea. You know I nearly held Lacey's baby this morning. She was super cute." He looked wistful. "To think I passed up that chance because I was worried about getting vomit or snot on my suit."

Emily snorted through her drink. "Oh my god, stop it! How did that work out for you?" she laughed until tears rolled down her cheeks as he grinned at her.

"I don't think it's nearly as funny as you do."

She continued giggling as he watched her with a mixture of amusement and bafflement. Finally she was able to draw a breath and take another sip of her drink.

They ate their meal, and then she asked the question that had been burning inside her ever since their most eventful interview wound up. "Who was in the photo in your office? That was yours wasn't it, not left behind by someone else?"

He quieted down and she focussed her attention on him. "That's my mum."

"You bring her photo everywhere you consult?"

"Not usually, but she passed away a few months ago."

"Oh, I'm sorry, Cooper." Instinctively she reached out and wrapped her hand around his. "That must have been awful." He looked at her hand but made no move to remove his own.

"It was. She used to call me over and over and I used to get annoyed with her. She'd been in a nursing home for the last twelve months. She'd call me, crying to 'go home' and begging me to come and get her. I wanted her to stay at my place but she needed round the clock care, which I couldn't provide. I planned to get a nurse but she had a fall before I could organise it and the hospital said the best place would be the home." The words were pouring out of him like he couldn't stop talking. Emily rubbed her finger over his thumb while he spoke and ignored the tear that glistened in the corner of his eye. "Anyway, I got a call one night. She got out of bed alone and had another fall. She hit her head and passed away."

"That's so sad."

"I feel really guilty, you know?" He looked up at her. "All those calls where I told her I loved her and we'd be together soon, and I didn't make enough time to visit her. I was busy with my life and there never seemed to be enough time. When I did visit sometimes she didn't know who I was and that was hard. She used to text me and it was just gibberish that I dutifully replied to." He sat back in his seat and

Emily looked hard at him for the first time. He'd aged since they'd been together. Nothing drastic, but the signs of stress and grief were etched into the tiny lines around his eyes and his mouth. No doubt he'd have had a few new grey hairs showing had he not been surfer-blonde.

She had her own dose of guilt to add to his, though. She suddenly knew who he'd been talking to the day she'd overheard those phone calls and watched him text all through lunch. There was no other woman. Emily had stupidly assumed the worst and she'd punished him for it. Worse than that, she'd punished herself. They'd had a promising relationship and it had been her who had ruined it. Not him.

In that moment, staring across the dinner table at him, she'd never been less proud of herself.

CHAPTER 8

"*T*here you go Andrew. Good boy. Stay on the stand."

Sasha and Jenny crowded into Emily's office. "Oh, it's been so long since you brought him in. Can we still feed him?"

"Yes, you can feed him. He has seeds there in his bowl."

"Hello Andrew." Sasha crooned to the bright green bird. "How are you doing?"

"Fiiiiiiiiine!" his low voice replied, and both women fell around laughing.

"Man, I love him. I wish I had a talking bird."

"It's a lifelong commitment. My mum taught him to speak twenty years ago when I was small. He may be inherited by my children, yet."

"Wow. That's so amazing. Here's a seed Andrew. Do you love seeds?"

"I love you!" he squawked and more laughter followed.

Soon he was imitating their laughter and Emily shooed them out of her office. "Enough, ladies. You can play with him later while I'm interviewing."

"Ooh, I'll be back. I remember in the days when this office was actually fun we could play with him for ages."

"Yes, but then I caught you teaching him to swear, remember Jenny?"

"I remember no such thing." She smirked and gave the bird a scratch on the neck before going back to her desk.

Emily cleared her email and checked her calendar for the day. Three interviews, as per Cooper's daily request. Plus she had a safety meeting, a short operations meeting and an appointment with a distributor. Lacey's first day was tomorrow and there was paperwork to be prepared for her, too.

Cooper wandered past the door. "You're in early."

"The early bird eats the worm!" Andrew screeched from the corner.

"Oh, hello Andrew." He approached the parrot and fed him a seed as Emily watched from the corner of her eye.

If only you knew the deep and meaningful conversations I had with Andrew about you after we broke up.

"Do you remember Cooper, Andrew?" he fed him another seed and looked over at Emily as she stared at her computer screen. "Do you think he remembers me?"

"Coooooopeeerrrrrrrrrr!"

"Ha! He can say my name!" he looked at her again. "How does he know that?"

"Coooooooperrrrrrrr is gone." Andrews voice was low and sad.

Uh-oh!

"Coooooooperrrrrrrr is a bad boy."

Emily pursed her lips and tapped out a reply to an email, while simultaneously wanting the ground to swallow her whole.

Shut up bird!

"Coooooooperrrrrrrr isn't coming back."

"Wow. He has all these phrases and he just puts my name at the start of each one, huh?"

"I told you he was chatty." She said brightly as she willed him to leave her office.

"Coooooooperrrrrrrr is banned from this house."

"Okay Andrew, I get the message. I thought you liked me dude." Cooper laughed and walked toward the door before addressing Emily. "I'll see you in the conference room at nine for our first adventure of the day?"

"Can't wait. Would you mind closing the door so that Andrew doesn't annoy everyone?"

"Sure." He glanced at the bird and she relaxed

knowing her purgatory would be over in just a second.

Before Cooper pulled the door completely shut, Andrew said in his saddest voice yet, "Coooooooperrrrrrrr broke my heart."

~

*E*mily avoided making eye contact with Cooper as they settled themselves at the boardroom table. Tiffany Kirven was seated opposite them, looking like she was born to work at Simpsons Stationery.

The introductions passed without incident and Emily launched into her planned questions. After several days of interviews she was already sick of the questions.

"What's your greatest weakness?"

"I used to struggle to be on time, but I've worked on that and now I give myself a lot more time to get places."

"Where do you see yourself in five years?"

"Well, I'd like to have learnt a lot about the business and be contributing to a lot of improvements. Personally, I hope I've managed to squeeze in a few more overseas trips by then."

Then the last question, delivered by Cooper. "Out of all the candidates, why should we hire you?" He held up a hand before Tiffany could answer. "Please don't say it's your birthday. We've already heard that one."

Emily burst out laughing and Cooper looked sideways at her. "She couldn't do that in the actual interview where that answer came up." he said, nodding his head toward her, and Tiffany joined in the laughter.

"It's definitely not my birthday, and I didn't meet any of the other candidates, but I can tell you that I enjoy my job, wherever I work. I've always found that I fit in well with other staff and I'm quick to learn any new tasks." She smiled at both of them in turn. "I take a lot of notes so I generally don't have to ask the same question over and over. You said you have quite a few roles to fill. I'd be an asset as I could be trained quickly and be less of a burden than someone less experienced."

"Perfect." When Emily spoke, relief was evident in her voice. "That's exactly what I like to hear. I think you'll be hearing from us very soon. You only have to give one week's notice, right?" She stood and stretched out her hand and Tiffany and Cooper followed her lead.

"Yes, I—" as she reached for Cooper's hand her skirt caught on the armrest of the chair she'd just vacated. She let out a loud 'oh' and then her arm shot up and she fell backward, almost in slow motion. Before Emily or Cooper could move, her chair toppled over and she was flailing with her legs across the chair; her skirt over her waist. Emily pushed Cooper aside and rushed to her rescue. The poor woman's underwear was showing and she tried to save her the embarrassment of Cooper having to assist.

"Are you okay?" she helped her to the side as Cooper righted the chair and they placed her back in it. "Does it hurt anywhere?"

"Oh my god I'm so embarrassed! No, I haven't hurt myself. My skirt caught on the seat and I suddenly had a huge muscle spasm in my shoulder. I don't even know how I jerked over in the chair like that. I'm so sorry—you must think I'm nuts."

Cooper patted her shoulder. "You're the least nuts of a large group that we've seen over the last few days. Please don't be embarrassed. We want you for this role and falling off your chair isn't going to change that."

"Thank you so much. You won't be sorry. I promise I'm not overly clumsy."

When Tiffany had been safely delivered to her car, Emily returned to the door of the conference room. "We don't need to go through the sheets do we? She's the best we've seen for the purchasing department."

"We should still do the sheets though. Stops anyone saying there was favouritism or something down the track." She filled in her sheet as fast as she could without sitting down in her chair. He glanced at it and compared it to his before nodding his head. "Great, we're in agreement."

She quickly moved to the door, letting him know she had a safety meeting to attend. She hoped he wouldn't mention the things that Andrew had said. They'd been doing so well these past weeks. Now the bird had made it awkward.

Well, you shouldn't have taught him to say those things!

~

"I think we should postpone this one."

"We can't. The guy is already here. Let's just see what kind of candidate we're likely to get, okay?" They were in Cooper's office, waiting for Sasha to let them know that their first pick for the operations manager role, Bill Gibbons, had arrived. "He could be great and blow you away."

"Maybe. I don't think we're ready for him, that's all."

"I've taken that on board. If he doesn't turn out to be great, we'll concentrate on the other positions. By the way, I've been thinking about the sales manager position." She reached behind her and pushed the door closed as she heard Andrew screeching on his stand. "I have no experience in hiring sales people, do you?"

"Some. Not a great deal." He admitted.

"Right. I think one of the reps we already have should be considered to be promoted to the sales manager job."

"Sounds fair. Can we advertise it internally and have people apply?"

"You took the words out of my mouth." The phone on Cooper's desk rang and Sasha announced the arrival of Mr Gibbons as Emily opened the door. "You meet him there, I'll be two seconds. I'm going to get Jenny to put the job out today via email."

Bill Gibbons was a stocky man who wore an impeccably cut suit and sported a severe crew cut. As they spoke to him they got the impression that he was a no nonsense type of man, who would not take kindly to people questioning his authority. His work history was varied and he had been an operations manager for the better part of twenty years. Emily felt there was something about his manner that might not fit in with their culture at Simpsons Stationery. She let Cooper take the lead throughout the interview, too, since it seemed he preferred speaking to Cooper than her.

When he left she waited for Cooper to return, for once not eager to escape. After that interview she was sure that Bill Gibbons was not the man for them.

Cooper closed the door and sat opposite her. "So, thoughts?"

"I didn't like him."

"That's very personal of you. How about for the role?"

She blushed and made a face at him. "I meant for the role. He seems a bit, what's the word? Mean."

"You're right. We need someone more personable. Possibly someone who doesn't mind actually speaking to a woman or making eye contact with her?"

"It wasn't my imagination, then? He didn't want to be questioned by me, did he?"

"That's how it appeared. You have a high ratio of female staff on this site. I don't think he's your guy."

They filled in their scoresheets, going through the motions so there would be a record of their decision. As Emily got up to leave, Cooper said, "Maybe we should have introduced him to Andrew. He could have told him, 'Bill isn't coming back!'"

She laughed and turned back, watching him smirk at her discomfort. "I'm sorry about the bird, Cooper. He just says any old thing and I really can't stop him"

He smiled at her. "Don't worry, I know it's not personal, though it's kind of freaky his word choices, isn't it?"

"You should try waking up in the middle of the night to hear him chatting to himself. I've been convinced more than once that someone was in the house. He even whispers; it makes him seem positively human."

If only he'd whispered earlier when he was telling all my secrets.

~

*A*t four o'clock the last thing Emily wanted to do was sit through another interview. She'd had a busy day, running from task to task and it looked like she'd be taking work home again tonight. When she went to the conference room Cooper was ready, looking like he'd just had a luxurious two-hour nap.

"Why do you look so chirpy?"

"Maybe because I have a normal workload and am not running myself ragged every night."

"You don't fool me. I've seen those spread sheets you've created since you've been here. Those things take hours—you have to be doing them at night since we're keeping you busy all day."

"True, but I don't count that as work too much. I enjoy it. Besides, what else do I have to do? Ed insisted I stay in the hotel even though I have a perfectly good house not that far away."

"You still live by the beach?"

"I do. I'm missing it, too. It's worth the drive just to be able to wake up to the salty smell of the ocean. Anyway, who's last on the list today?"

"Lucy Jones will be here in a few minutes. She's the one who wrote a note on her resume that she was interested in either the customer service job or the purchasing role."

"She's keen."

The door opened and Sasha announced Lucy's arrival. She stepped aside and one of the most beautiful women Emily had ever seen swept into the room. The door closed and they caught sight of Sasha rolling her eyes before it shut completely.

After the initial pleasantries they found that Lucy did most of the talking. One question could get her chattering away for minutes on end without appearing to take a breath. Cooper seemed rapt in her answers and made furious notes on his computer as Emily watched with an interested smirk.

"Uh... would it be possible to get a drink of water?" Lucy's round eyes blinked at Cooper.

"Of course. Let me get you one." He jumped from his chair and headed for the door. "You keep talking, I won't be long."

The door clicked shut and Lucy turned to Emily. "He seems so lovely. What a shame he's not a full-time employee here."

"Yes, a real shame."

"Do you know if he's single? He's dishy!"

"Pardon?"

"Is he seeing anyone? Do you think I have a chance? Since we wouldn't be working together, it would be okay." It wasn't a question—she didn't appear to be asking for permission.

"That's something you'll have to pursue outside this interview, I'm afraid."

Manicured fingernails tapped on the table and Emily decided in that second that Lucy Jones would get a job at Simpsons Stationery over her dead body.

"I'll have to make sure I—" Cooper returned with the water and handed it to her. "Thank you so much. That was so sweet of you." She definitely batted her eyelashes that time and Emily felt a flush creep up her body. "I just want you to know, Mr Jackson, that I'll do anything to secure this role." More eyelash flickering. "If there's anything that would guarantee me the position, I'd be more than happy to oblige."

Is she suggesting what I think she is?

The eye contact Lucy was lavishing on Cooper was uncomfortable to watch and Emily had had enough. She quickly wound up the interview and made sure she was the one to escort Lucy downstairs. As she said her goodbyes Lucy slipped a piece of paper into her hand. "Can you give this to Cooper? I don't know if you saw it but I definitely got the vibe that he wanted my number."

She handed it back with her best icy stare. "We have your resume Ms Jones. If *Mr Jackson*," she emphasised his name, "wants to call you he can get the number from there."

She stomped back upstairs, cursing the day she'd ever laid eyes on Cooper Jackson. Why should she care if he dated Lucy? What difference would it make to her if he started seeing someone?

A whole damn lot of difference, if she were to be one hundred percent honest with herself.

Cooper met her at the conference room door. "Phew! How was her form? Was she offering to sleep with me, just to get a job in customer service?" he laughed loudly and Emily stared at him.

"You weren't interested? You seemed captivated by those lashes."

"Hell no! She's totally not my type. Waaaaay too brazen for me."

"She asked me to give you her number but I refused. I told her we have it on her resume so she'll probably be waiting for your call."

He laughed again and they walked toward their offices. "She'll be waiting a very long time for that call. I assume she's a no on your list of applicants?"

"She's a big no. Anyone who subtly propositions the person interviewing them isn't going to work here."

"Fair enough."

Faintly, from the direction of her office, Emily heard Andrew start up. "Coooooooperrrrrrrr can't be trusted!" he sang out as she coughed and tried to cover the sound.

"You talk to the bird at home quite a bit, huh?"

"Shhh… Andrew. People are working."

"Don't shush me! I'll tell your father!" he squawked, bobbing up and down on his perch.

"Andrew, please. Cooper might send you home."

"Cooper, schmooper." He shrieked, and then he was off, saying all the phrases he knew as fast as he could, and all at the top of his voice. "He broke my heart, he's not coming back, he's a bad man, Cooper is gone. Gone in the head. Gone from the bed. We'll burn the bed Andrew. Andrew is better than Cooper. Cooper smells. Cooper is poop. Cooper can't sing. Andrew can siiiiiiiing!"

Emily squeezed her eyes shut. She'd brought Andrew to work dozens of times over the years and he usually sat happily in the corner telling the girls he loved them and asking them to fill up his seeds. This time he'd decided to repeat every word she'd ever said to him about Cooper. Good and bad.

CHAPTER 9

$\mathcal{E}$mily felt bad about leaving Andrew at home the next day, but with the office bubbling away on their newest gossip, she didn't want to risk a repeat of his naughty antics. Cooper had kept his good humour about it, but there was only so much one person could bear before they didn't find it funny anymore. With her days filled with interviews and every interruption imaginable, Emily didn't need the distraction the bird offered, anyway.

She was the first one to arrive in the office and she enjoyed an hour of peace and quiet before the day truly began. When she was summoned to reception to collect their first interviewee she smirked at the conversation she overheard.

"I had to bring my cat along since I'm having a real estate inspection today and I need to hide him from the agent. He's not on the lease yet, so they can't find him there."

Sasha's uncertain voice carried around the corner. "Uh okay. Just pop him here under my desk. He won't do anything disgusting like spray me will he?"

"Oh no dear. I brought him in the cage so he can't get out. He's been desexed and he quite likes women, anyway. He'll be quiet as a church mouse and I'll get him back just as soon as I can." He pushed the carrier under her desk and stood up with a worried expression. "You don't think this will reflect badly on me here, do you, because I'm essentially lying to my agent?

"I won't tell if you don't," Sasha said, and she winked at him as Emily walked around the corner.

"I imagine leaving your pet in the hot car while you come in for a job interview would reflect a lot worse on you than tucking him under our receptionist's desk," she said as her first victim of the day paled in front of her. "Don't worry," she waved for him to follow her upstairs, "it's fine. She had to look after a baby last week, I'm sure she can manage your cat."

They kept the interview short and an hour later escorted him downstairs to collect his adored pet. He'd talked about the cat way too much while he was with them and it soon became apparent he wouldn't be a good fit for their team.

As soon as he was out the door, Cooper started up

the stairs and leaned over the bannister to talk to Emily. "Both the other interviews are scheduled after lunch. How do you feel about discussing improvement plans for Simpsons that you can implement once you're fully staffed?"

"No problem. Let me just get a drink of water and I'll be right up."

They spent four hours going over the business goals that were already in place and the ten-year plan the directors had published as their upcoming vision for the company. Cooper was impressed with the details that had been recorded against the goals and he suggested only a couple of tweaks, much to Emily's relief.

She'd had a loose plan in the back of her head that as soon as they had a full complement of staff, they'd get straight back to implementing their long-term plans. Of course, that would be up to the new operations manager. She'd be firmly back in her human resources box when that happened, and probably wouldn't have as much of a say anymore.

The phone rang in the conference room and Sasha announced their one o'clock appointment had arrived. Trixie Smith appeared nervous as she sat across from them and Emily eventually asked her if everything was okay.

"I'm so sorry if I seem a bit flustered. This is my third interview today and they've been kind of crazy."

"In what way?"

She bit her lip, "I'm not sure if I should say. It's not usual interview conversation."

"No pressure," Cooper said. "We've had some pretty interesting experiences ourselves recently." He smiled at her and watched as she did a good job of pretending she had relaxed. Her fingers tapping the side of her chair said otherwise, though.

"Well, the first position today was not what it was advertised as and when I left the gentleman interviewing insisted that he would drop me wherever I wanted to go."

"Wow, that's bad. You poor thing."

"Yeah. I caught the bus but he sat with me at the stop until it arrived. It shook me up a bit, I have to confess."

"I promise that's not going to happen here. We pride ourselves on being professional."

She visibly relaxed and they launched into the interview. Trixie was interesting and gave appropriate answers to all the questions. By the time they were finished she was joking with them and any sign of her previous nervousness was gone.

As they shook her hand at the door Cooper said, "Did you want to tell us what happened to you at your second interview that was so bad?" he laughed.

She stepped out of the conference room and smiled at them. "You won't believe it. The interviewer wanted to read my palm!"

~

*T*rue to form, the last applicant of the day was the one that left them both reeling from the experience. Jack Steele settled himself in the office and appeared enthusiastic about the sales position he was interviewing for.

"Your resume says you've worked in sales ever since you left school. That's a long time to be in one type of role." Emily asked the first question.

"I really like sales. I like being out of the office, meeting the customers, almost becoming their friends, if you like."

"Do you want to advance from the salesman role at any point?"

"Not at the moment. There's a whole lot of paperwork and red tape once you're managing other people. I think I can leave that for a few years yet."

"Our role would require you to travel. You'll be away most weeks for at least three days. Is there any reason that would be a problem for you?"

"Oh, hell no!" Emily felt the familiar tap on her foot. "The more time spent away from home the better, you know. I can't be nagged by the wife if I'm not there, can I?" He laughed at his own statement and eagerly awaited the next question. From the look on his face he thought he was acing the interview.

"Is there any reason we shouldn't hire you?"

"I can be loud and boisterous at the office Christmas party!" he laughed again and slapped his knee before becoming serious again. "You do have a Christmas party, right? Everything put on by the company?"

Cooper shifted in his chair and Emily tried hard not to smirk. After sitting through so many interviews with him, she was intimately familiar with his body language. The fact that his body language often said he wanted her to give in and go home with him was irrelevant. She could tell he'd had enough of this interviewee and would soon wind up the questions. Unfortunately Jack didn't have the same advantage and he continued speaking, unaware what he was doing to his chances of employment with Simpsons.

"Do you guys do Friday drinks? My last employer put drinks on for us every Friday afternoon and it was a great way of bonding with the team. If you don't have it, you should." He grinned at Cooper, "Of course I have to get a taxi home those nights. Being responsible and all after I get hammered is something I'm great at. Doesn't impress the missus the next day when she drops me back, but I'm all about safety."

"That's good." Cooper's tone said he was giving anything but a good impression. "Do you have any other questions for us? Something we haven't covered?"

"Well, you didn't answer my question about the

Christmas party." He looked straight at Cooper. "Is it paid for by the company?"

Emily answered before Cooper could speak, "Our Christmas party is definitely put on by the company."

"Oh great. Those ones where you have to pay yourself, or put money in a box each week to go toward the party are lame. You work hard all year, you want to be rewarded with a piss-up, you know?"

"I do, indeed. Let's worry about the hiring part before we get to the Christmas celebrations, shall we? Anything else before we wind this up?"

"Yes, I was wondering what other perks you offer? Can I salary sacrifice to save on tax? Or do you have free meals at lunchtime? Free mobile phone or parking?" he held up his fingers and ticked the items off one by one. "Some places they had free vending machines or a free fruit basket you could help yourself to. A cake on your birthday. So much great stuff, you know?"

Emily had had enough. "We'd probably discuss those things at a second interview."

Disappointment filled his face. "Oh, okay then. I'm probably not your best guy if there aren't a lot of perks. I've worked out you can get up to five percent of your salary in free stuff if you choose the right employer."

"Is that right?" Emily stood up and Cooper followed suit. "How interesting. I'll take you downstairs and we'll be in touch within the next week to let you know our decision." She steered him toward the door and down the stairs as he continued to chatter about the free things some employers gave out. When she finally said goodbye to him at the front door she had a throbbing headache.

CHAPTER 10

*A*ndrea checked her reflection in the mirror of the elevator that she was lucky enough to ride alone. The walk from the car had been hot and she was pleased to see she wasn't sweating too much. She welcomed the coolness of the foyer as she made her way to the bank of elevators. This interview needed to go well for her.

A dream job was what this business offered and it was the one she wanted above all others. She'd be an executive assistant to the director and have her own private office next to his. The role involved a small amount of international travel and that part interested her a great deal. The time away from Lori would be hard, but they'd discussed it and decided to try it out. The initial meeting had gone well and she was confident she was close to being offered the position. The person on the phone said if she was successful today, and they wanted her for to start, the next step was a medical. If she passed she'd be offered the position in writing.

Just before two o'clock she approached the reception desk and let them know she had arrived. The receptionist gave her an apologetic look and informed her that Mr North was running about half an hour later. He'd requested she be shown to the conference room to wait. She passed the time scanning through Facebook on her phone and craning to hear when he was coming so she could quickly slip it into her bag. If she'd known she would have to wait so long she'd have tucked a book in to her handbag before leaving home.

She was idly sorting through her handbag when she realised she didn't have her keys. She pushed the contents around a couple of times, but they weren't there.

An image of her rushing to get out of the car returned to her and she realised where they were—dangling in the ignition of the damn car! The blood drained from her face as she realised what she'd done, and what a pain in the ass getting them out was going to be. She'd need to call roadside assistance. On the hottest day of the year, too.

Thirty-five minutes later her prospective boss bustled into the room. She could see he'd rushed to the office. He was sweating and as she sat down again after shaking his hand her eyes fell on his zipper. Not because she was looking there, but because his white shirt poked through the gap, where his zipper was very clearly down. As he settled himself opposite she spied a smudge of lipstick across the side of his collar.

He apologised several times for being late, explaining he'd had 'something unforeseen' to attend to.

Unforeseen! Ha! Is that what they're calling it now?

She ran over the previous interview in her head as he pulled out his laptop to take notes. He'd been nothing but professional. They'd discussed the role, what would be required of her and the starting salary. There'd been no indication that he might be as unprofessional as he appeared right now. Anxiety crept into her belly. Hopefully this wasn't the kind of role where she'd be expected to cover for him each time he had an 'unforeseen' appointment pop up.

Shoving her doubts aside, and trying to forget about the keys, she threw herself into the interview. Knowing she had the opportunity to find work with Emily made it a little easier to relax but no matter what they discussed, or how many questions he asked her, she just could not make herself look him in the eye.

The lipstick on his collar would draw her attention, she knew, and she would immediately give herself away. He was talking so much and glancing at his laptop screen that he probably hadn't noticed anyway.

"Well that all seems great, Andrea. Can I ask you one more thing, though?"

"Sure."

"Well, you seem a bit awkward this time around. I thought we got along pretty well last time but today you're less enthusiastic. Is something wrong? Have you changed your mind about working for me?"

"No, of course not. I really want this position." She still couldn't look up and she stared at his hands on the table. "It will be quite awkward to tell you what's wrong and I wouldn't want it to harm my chances at getting the job."

"Andrea, please look at me." His voice had an air of command and she reminded herself that he was her prospective employer. She grit her teeth and slowly raised her eyes, blinking as the lipstick smudge caught her eye. "There, that wasn't so hard was it? Now tell me, what's happened to upset you?"

"I'm not upset. I just… " Her words died away and she had an overwhelming desire to burst out laughing. "You have a little something…" she motioned at her own collar and his eyes widened. He wiped at the side of his neck and she rolled her eyes and gave up. "You have lipstick on your collar. A large amount of red lipstick. And while I'm busy ensuring I don't get this job your fly is also undone." She finally smiled at him, shaking her head as his face turned pale. "I'm so sorry. I tried to ignore it."

He ran his palm over his face and hung his head in front of him. When he raised it she could see he wanted to laugh. "I'm the one who should apologise. I'm truly sorry." He sighed, making no move to fix his zipper.

Thank goodness I can't see it under the desk!

"I told my wife I was interviewing you again today. She's a bit worried about my new assistant, since I had to fire the old one for hitting on me. She called me for lunch and one thing led to another. I guess she was trying to make a point."

"Point taken."

"You and me both! This is so unprofessional and I'm so sorry to put you in this position. I want you to take the job but I'll understand if you decline after what's happened here today."

"I guess your wife wants you to take on someone a bit older."

"If she had her way I'd employ her grandmother." He laughed and Andrea quickly joined in. "Honestly, it's the overseas travel we'll be doing that's got her in a twist. I told her she should come along but our kids are both small. Makes it hard for her to get away to come with me."

"That's understandable. I am interested in this job and I think I'd be great at it. Maybe we can organise to meet each other as soon as I start."

"That's a great idea. You can thank her for making this the most horrific job interview you've had to endure."

"Oh, I will, don't worry."

"I'm pleased we've settled that and I'm really pleased you confessed. I was starting to think you were trying to put me off so I wouldn't choose you."

"Not at all." Andrea shook his hand and rose from her seat as he continued speaking.

"I'll get HR to call you when they have a date for the medical."

"Perfect."

He pushed his chair back and she suddenly panicked over what she would see should he stand. "No! Please stay there and let me see myself out."

He laughed and nodded as he raised his hands. "I'm sorry! I'm sorry! Yes, I'll stay right here."

～

*A*ndrea escaped down the elevator as fast as she could. Her face burned with embarrassment as she walked the two long blocks back to the car. Not even the knowledge that she had the job could put a spring in her step or stop the heat in her face.

That was horrific. The worst thing I've ever experienced. I'm going home to relax—nothing will ever beat this. Wait until I tell the girls!

The sight of her car was a welcome relief. She'd parked in a dodgy side street that had a history of having cars towed for no good reason. At least she wouldn't have to add a battle with a council inspector or the towing company to her list of tasks today. All she needed to do was wait for assistance, get her keys out and head home. As she neared the car, something seemed different about it, though. Her eyes widened as she stood beside it, finally realising what had happened.

To top off her perfect day, someone had stolen the hubcaps!

~

"*H*ey Andrea!" Emily gave her friend a big hug. "Congratulations on getting the job. I'm bummed we won't be getting you, though!"

"I'm in high demand, what can I say." They laughed and settled themselves around the table for dinner. "Let's order and then I'll regale you with the ordeal I had to go through to get this job. You won't believe it."

"After the week I've had, I'll believe anything. Hi Luke, I didn't know you were coming."

"Jordan lets me out of the house sometimes." He winced as she elbowed him in the ribs. "Mostly so I can walk Rex."

"Sure, sure. Except I already know that Jordan

just moved in with you, so I don't think you're doing it too tough buddy."

"There are no secrets with you girls," he muttered as he surveyed the menu and squeezed Jordan's leg under the table.

"Emily, did you invite Cooper?"

"No, why?"

"Because he just walked in." They all turned to look as the waiter showed Cooper to a table behind them. He was seated at a table for two and Emily quickly turned back to face the group.

"Maybe he has a date," Luke mused.

"I don't care. Please don't give me a blow-by-blow account of his night. We came here to have some fun!"

"I think he's on his own. He only got one menu." Luke continued to relay what Cooper was doing. "He's about to order. We should invite him to sit with us." Jordan thumped him on the thigh under the table. "Ow! Come on Jordan, I liked Cooper, I wouldn't mind if he joined us."

"Fine!" Emily snapped at him as she stood and threw her napkin on the table. "You're making so much noise it will be awkward if he sees us now." She turned and approached Cooper's table, excusing herself as the waiter was poised to take his order. "Cooper." She said and his head snapped up, his eyes meeting hers as that gorgeous smile stretched across his face. "If you're here alone, would you like to join our table? I'm here with all the gang." She indicated Luke, Jordan, Shelly, Boyd and Andrea watching behind her and each of them gave a wave.

"I see we have our privacy," he joked as he handed his menu to the waiter. "I'd love to join you, if you don't mind."

"I don't mind. Plus Luke is badgering me. Apparently he likes you." She turned back to her own table. "Who knew?" she threw over her shoulder.

There was room at the end of the table for Cooper but of course her friends hastily rearranged themselves and everyone moved down one spot, like a crazy rendition of the mad hatter's tea party. She sure felt like Alice as she took her place and Cooper slipped in beside her. She was out of her depth and in unknown territory. Did she treat him like a workmate or a friend? Like her ex or just a guy they'd invited to join them for dinner? They'd spent a lot of time together over the past few weeks and she had to admit the old feelings she had for him had been trying to break through. She'd tramped them down each time, but it got harder and harder to resist the more time they spent together. Now she'd have to endure another night sitting next to him.

He leaned in and spoke quietly, "I'm glad to see you're not working tonight."

"I decided to have the night off. Now we have a few more staff I have some breathing room. Thank you for that. It was the right decision to focus on those roles first. At least for me." She smiled and passed him the water jug. "Make sure you talk to Luke tonight. He appears to have developed a man-crush." They both laughed and Cooper turned to talk to Luke, while Emily was reminded of the night in the pub all those months ago when they'd all been together. She'd had fun watching Cooper joke with her friends. Tonight seemed like it could turn out the same way.

She considered that true, right up until the moment she heard Cooper say to Luke, "Let me tell you what Emily's bird screamed throughout the office a few days ago."

CHAPTER 11

"*D*o we really have to do this?"

"We do. Why are you chicken all of a sudden?"

"I like the interviewing part. I don't enjoy telling people they no longer have a job."

"The great Cooper Jackson is scared of firing someone. That surprises me."

"I'm not scared." He scribbled on his notepad. "It's just that I've never actually let anyone go before."

"Ha! Really?"

"Really. I choose staff carefully and they usually leave of their own accord. Mostly for better opportunities."

"How many staff do you have, anyway?" Emily sat down next to him as she sorted through the file in front of her.

"Only two. I have a personal assistant and I outsource my accounts. So the bookkeeper isn't even staff I guess."

"Don't worry about it. I'll do all the talking. Remember, we're doing this first so we can do the good meeting afterward."

He grinned at her. "I noticed you set them up like that. You left the positive one for last on purpose?"

"I did. I don't like the bad meetings to linger so I always follow up with something positive.

"Clever."

"I try."

"So, no Andrew today?"

"Hell no!" The words were out before Emily considered them and she rolled her eyes at Cooper. "After the other week I think I may ban him from the office."

"He sure was chatty. Right up until the moment you took him out to the car."

"You heard that?"

He laughed as he said the words that turned her face crimson. "I'll never forget the sound of his shrieks echoing up the staircase and down the corridor. There's something quite alarming about a parrot screaming 'take Andrew back! Andrew is decent! Not like Coooooopppperrrrr!'"

*M*ick Gordon from the warehouse took the news well and Emily and Cooper quickly moved to their next meeting. They'd asked Heather to come upstairs at eleven o'clock and when she arrived she was a bundle of nerves. News had spread about their task from the morning and she looked like she was on the verge of tears as she steeled herself for whatever they were about to say.

"First of all Heather," Emily began, "please relax. We're not finishing you up."

Heather let out a pent up breath and flopped forward in her chair. "Oh thank goodness. I was so worried when I heard you let Mick go this morning."

"Mick wasn't performing and he'd already had two written warnings." Cooper informed her. "You haven't had any warnings have you, Heather?"

"No of course not." She was shocked that he'd even suggested such a thing.

"Great. Then you can relax."

Emily gave his foot a tap under the table. "Please ignore Cooper being so flippant, and let me explain why you're here. We've been looking at everyone who works at Simpsons and laying out the tasks that they do." Heather nodded. "We want to offer you some extra training because I know that sometimes you struggle with the computer and the various programs."

"I'm sure I can do better to learn them." She

spoke like she still suspected this was some sort of test.

"I know you can but we want you to learn them properly from a trainer, not through us showing you a keystroke every second month because we just realised you don't know it. You're a valuable member of staff. You're friendly, you help others with their boring tasks when they get behind and your own work is great. We want to help you to be better so that you have a long future with us."

A tear rolled down Heather's cheek and Cooper sat up, alarmed. She sniffled and then pulled a tissue out of her sleeve, making Emily smile. "Thank you so much!" she said as she wiped her eyes and then dabbed her nose. "I was so worried coming up here, but you've made me feel so valued."

"You're very welcome." Emily pushed some papers toward her. "Here are the course details we have for you. You'll see there's more than one. Talk to your department and let me know which dates suit you best." Heather took the papers and got up from her chair. Emily rose and walked her to the door. "Can you do one more thing for me?"

"Yes, of course."

"Can you make sure you let everyone know those are happy tears? I don't want a revolt in my office when they think we fired our most loved staff member!"

"*T*hat went well." Cooper followed Emily to her office and lingered in the doorway as she sat at her desk. The sight of him lounging there was becoming familiar to her, now that he'd being doing it for several weeks. She tore her eyes away and focussed on her computer monitor. "How do you feel about closing the site for an entire day and running a team building exercise of some sort?"

Her head snapped up. "That's pretty extreme, but we could make it work. As long as it's not lame. No high ropes courses or I'm out."

He laughed and pushed off from the doorframe. "Let's talk about it later, but I have some ideas that you'll like. It needs to be a day that feels like a reward for your people, not a punishment where they'd rather have had a day off work."

"Sounds good." She went back to her email, but he didn't return to his office.

"Will you have dinner with me?"

"Nope."

"Please. I believe I owe you a thank you."

"No, you don't owe me anything. Especially after the way that Andrew behaved the other day. It's bad enough that everyone has worked out that we dated a few times. I'm going to kill that bird."

"So it wasn't you who replaced the photo frame

for me?" He took two steps to his office and quickly returned to hold it up.

"Yes, it was me, but I don't need a thank you."

"It was nice of you."

"So, I'm nice. I still don't need a thank you."

"How about if we make it a working dinner?"

She sighed and closed her eyes for a moment, before turning toward him. "You don't give up do you?"

"Not when I want something." His eyes bored into hers, telegraphing a double meaning to his words.

"You promised Ed."

"That was a mistake. I'm considering retracting it."

"You can't do that!" Now he had her full attention. "I don't want you making work even more complicated."

"I guess that's a yes to dinner, then." He smirked and stepped away from the door, cheering quietly and high-fiving himself all the way back to his office.

~

*E*mily was determined to keep their dinner focussed on work and not give him any leeway to start a personal discussion. She insisted on taking her car to dinner and promised to drop him at his hotel afterward. As she drove in silence, she mulled over the short talk she'd had with Jenny after Andrew had outed her to the entire office.

"He's so sexy. No wonder you dated him."

"Shhh… Jenny. No one was supposed to know."

"Well, Andrew screwed that up, didn't he? Who knew he'd start saying all that stuff?"

"Don't remind me. Cooper has been very good about it."

"I've seen the way Cooper watches you Emily. He wants another chance, I'd bet my house on it."

"No, he doesn't. We're working together for a few more weeks, then everything will go back to normal." She'd nodded, to convince herself more than anyone.

Jenny had actually put her finger up and tapped her on the forehead. "Hello! You're making a mistake. Guys like Cooper Jackson don't come along every day. Grab him before someone else does. Someone like that Lucy woman that you interviewed."

Emily laughed. "He said he wasn't interested but I did point out he could get her number any time he liked from her resume."

"Well, he can't because I shredded it." Jenny grinned, pleased with the shocked look on Emily's face. "And, Sasha has been intercepting all the calls she's made since her interview."

"She called him?"

"She did. More than once. I told her last time that Cooper had moved to another office."

"That's evil of you."

"Yep. You're welcome. So, as I was saying, grab him while he's here. No one in their right mind would let a sexy surfer dude, who's well spoken and a great guy slip through their fingers."

She shook the memory away and pulled into a vacant parking space. When they were settled in the restaurant she pulled out her computer, silently communicating to him that she was here for work. Her eyes focussed on her computer screen while Cooper frowned at her. "Can you put the laptop away? We're here for dinner."

"You said a working dinner," she reminded him.

"So I lied. I expected you to give in gracefully when I said it was work-related and then be bowled over by my charm and let me get away with it. But no, here we are discussing the finer points and making it awkward."

She sighed and closed the laptop before slipping it into her bag. "Why couldn't you just let me go home?"

His exasperation was plain for anyone to see as he hissed at her, "Because I don't want you to go home unless I can come with you. I'd let you go home, if home was my place by the beach and you were moving in." He relaxed a little and sat back in his chair, his emotions still out of control. "I'd even let you bring Andrew, if we could tape his nasty mouth shut."

His vicious words about her pet made Emily giggle and soon the small eruption became outright laughter. Cooper's face softened and he soon joined in. The waiter approached their table and then detoured to a different one when he saw them guffawing and slapping each other's arms as they shrieked.

"Oh, man, that bird will be the death of me! I've never heard him say so many words in one day in his entire life. If I had a housemate I'd have accused them of setting me up and teaching him what to do."

"The look on Jenny's face when you took him out to the car and he just kept screaming about me was priceless. She didn't know where to look when I passed her desk."

"I'm not happy that they all know about us."

"No, it wasn't the best way for them to find out. I sent Ed an email, just so you're aware. In case it becomes an issue."

She immediately sobered. "Did he reply?"

"He did."

"And?"

Cooper pursed his lips and looked directly at her. "You won't like it."

"Oh, no. What?"

"He said he couldn't give a shit." He grinned at her as she swatted at his arm again. "Said you deserved to be happy and if ever two people were made for each other it was us."

"Wow. That's a bit sloppy for Ed."

"I know, I was surprised myself. He said if it went bad he would seek my immediate removal. Emily is more important to the company than some horny consultant, were his exact words. It means it's okay."

"No, it's still not okay."

He groaned. "Will it be okay in November when I've completed my mission?"

She watched him, watching her, and was lost for words. What do you say to a man you really like, or suspect you might even be in love with, when he asks you that? How do you tell him you're scared of being hurt again, even though you know it was entirely your fault last time? How do you confess the awful and selfish reason that you broke it off?

You don't.

"I'm not sure that's what I want."

Much better to bluff your way through.

"Bullshit. I won't push it tonight, but I know you want me as much as I want you."

Damn.

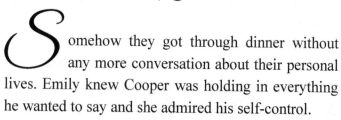

Somehow they got through dinner without any more conversation about their personal lives. Emily knew Cooper was holding in everything he wanted to say and she admired his self-control.

Time to get him home before I lose mine.

As they got into the car to start the short drive to his hotel, he surprised her with a question. "What's something in your life you still want to achieve?"

"That's a weird question. Why do you want to know?"

"I'm just making small talk. We can discuss how much you want me if you'd prefer."

"No, I think a discussion about my life goals is much safer." She pulled out into the deserted street before answering. "I'd like to see the Northern Lights. I'm fascinated by them and by all the photos I've seen of see through hotel-type igloos. They're definitely on my bucket list."

"Nice." He smiled to himself in the dark. "I wouldn't mind seeing those either. You know you can see them in Tasmania at certain times of the year."

"No way!"

"Yep, it's true. I'll show you the Aurora Australis, otherwise known as the Southern Lights, on my phone tomorrow. Not to move on to discuss anything too personal, but once I've talked you into dating me again, I'll take you on holiday to see them."

The traffic light turned green and she edged forward, glancing at him as she drove slowly. "That's totally not true! You promised no personal talk, anyway! Oh—" she slammed on the brakes, suddenly realising that the traffic light had not turned green, but was still red, and they were now parked in the middle of the intersection. "It wasn't my light!"

Traffic to her right started to move forward and she panicked that they were about to be the cause of an accident. Quickly checking to her left she tramped hard on the accelerator and rushed the car out of the intersection.

"What the hell was that?" Cooper said, his wide-eyed stare settling on her.

"Oh my God! I was sure the light turned green, but it wasn't mine. That junction can be confusing but I could have killed us!" She drove slowly up the street, pulling in big breaths, noticing that her hands shook on the steering wheel. "I'm so sorry."

Cooper let out a short laugh. "I'll have to remember not to declare my intentions while you're driving. I promise to stick to discussions about the weather from now on."

She laughed, but it was a sound devoid of mirth. "I can't believe I did that. I've only gone through two red lights in my entire life and that was the second. Wow. Just, wow." She glanced in the rear view mirror and watched the traffic move slowly through the junction behind them. "We are so lucky it's late."

"It's okay. Just take it easy and we'll make it home alive."

"Oh no." Her eyes flicked from the rear mirror and back to the road in front. "I think that's a police car."

"Oh sure. Funny, funny. This is not a time for jokes."

"It's not a joke, Cooper." Worry crinkled at the edge of her eyes. "I recognise the shape of the wagon. Just wait and the lights will go on any second. Make sure you have your seatbelt on." She turned right at the next traffic light, being careful to indicate and still watching the car in her mirror. As predicted the red and blue lights started flashing and the car pulled in behind them. "See? Oh my goodness, I'm going to get a fine."

She didn't stop the car immediately as they were on a two-lane road, instead taking the next residential street on the left and pulling to a careful stop behind a parked car. Cooper turned in his seat and watched as officers got out of each side of the car, torches flashing. "Oh, you've got two of them interested. They'll be worrying about who's in the car since we didn't pull over straight away."

"Don't say that." Emily opened her door and didn't miss the quick step backward the officer took.

He thinks I'm a threat and I'm getting out of the car!

"Hi there." He shone the light in her face as his partner shone his in Cooper's window. "Do you know why we've pulled you over this evening?"

"I do, and my window is broken, that's why I'm opening my door."

"Why have we stopped you?" he asked, ignoring her statement about the door.

As Emily's mouth opened, her brain chose that

exact moment to take a holiday. "Because I must be on some kind of *drug* or something, and that was not my green light back there!"

"That's correct. Do you have your licence on you?"

"I do."

She picked up her handbag from the floor and Cooper whispered to her, "You just told a police officer you're on drugs!" She glared at him in the darkness and concentrated on getting her licence as he held in his giggles.

"Oh my goodness, we were talking and laughing and then I realised I was out in the middle of the intersection and my light was actually red," she babbled as she dug around in her purse for her licence, ignoring Cooper's hysterical choking sounds. "I just rushed to get us out of harm's way before any cars could move through." She handed him her licence, "Here you go."

"Thanks." As he lifted it to look, she reached out and snatched it out of his hand.

"Oh I'm sorry. That's my banking card!"

"Well, I'm not interested in that tonight." His answer almost made her laugh, but she kept it in, unlike Cooper who now started laughing outright beside her.

"Would you shut up?" she hissed at him as she finally found her licence and handed it to the officer.

He shone his light on the plastic ID card and she

knew exactly what was coming next. "This is a Queensland licence."

"Yes."

"How long have you lived in Victoria?"

From beside her, Cooper said between giggles, "Two years," and the officer raised his eyebrows.

She smiled at him and tried to look vague. "Umm... maybe a year and a half. Two years, or so?" Her tone rose at the end like a question and she willed herself not to turn around and look at the other officer, who was now checking her tyres by torchlight.

"Do you realise you are required to change your licence to a Victorian one after," he looked at his partner who had appeared with a breath testing kit, "it's three months isn't it?"

Oh god, I'm behaving so insanely they think I'm drunk!

"Yep, three months is the deadline," his partner agreed and handed him the package.

"Oh, really? I didn't know that." *A lie.* "I even flew to Queensland when it expired last year so I wasn't driving unlicensed." *Not a lie.*

She ignored Cooper as he informed her in a low voice near her shoulder that she'd be getting a second fine for that oversight.

God I wish you weren't here to witness this!

"I guess I'm committing all kinds of crimes tonight," she said with a laugh, as she smiled up at the officer and Cooper finally lost his mind in the passenger seat. She elbowed him and kept her eyes on the uniformed man in front of her. "Please excuse my workmate. Can you hear him laughing at me?"

The officer handed the licence to his partner who returned to the vehicle. Without smiling at all he instructed her to blow into the yellow tube. She followed his instructions, almost losing her breath at the end. Cooper's giggling was rubbing off on her and she experienced an overwhelming desire to laugh. From the look on the officer's face laughing was the wrong thing to do, so she bit her lip and waited to hear how much her moment of inattention at the traffic lights was going to cost.

The officer announced her alcohol reading was zero and both officers returned to their vehicle while she glared at Cooper. "Would you stop it? I'm probably going to get eight hundred dollars worth of fines."

He ignored her and continued laughing, sliding down in his seat and slapping his knee. He gasped as he spoke, "You said you were on drugs to a cop! Then you told him you were committing all kind of crimes! I can't believe you said that." He continued laughing and she shook her head as the officer approached her door again.

"Well," he started, and she braced herself for the bad news, "It's your lucky night. The fine for running the red light is around four hundred dollars and it's about the same for not changing your licence over.

However," he paused for effect and Emily held her breath, "I'm able to let you off with a warning tonight."

She let out her breath in a whoosh as Cooper finally stopped laughing. "Thank you so much!"

"Drive carefully and have a good evening."

"Thank you! I will! Straight home!"

She pulled the door closed and ignored Cooper as he said, "Ooh, another fib! You're on fire tonight!"

CHAPTER 12

The next two weeks saw a flurry of new staff activity at Simpsons Stationery. Emily was thrilled that every person they'd chosen had agreed to take up their roles. She'd expected at least one to call and say they got a better offer elsewhere, but all the new starts went smoothly, and for that she was grateful.

Her workload gradually decreased and she was able to return many of the reporting functions she'd taken on to their respective departments. She still needed to complete the work of the operations manager, since Cooper had been stalling on any more interviews for that role, but she finally had some time to herself each night.

Her new assistant was a godsend and Jenny was also able to return to many of the high-level tasks she'd been doing before their shakeup.

Ed had even called Emily to let her know that the regulator had advised they would likely face smaller fines as they'd taken such decisive action when they'd discovered the dishonest behaviour of their staff.

The only cloud on her horizon was Cooper. They'd had dinner two more times recently and he hadn't let up with his insistence that they should date. He'd taken to touching her on the back whenever he was close, sending her funny emails, and had kept up his habit of nudging her foot under the table whenever something amused him in a meeting.

She liked the small touches—liked every moment they spent together. Her resolve was weakening day by day, and he knew it.

Today they'd closed the site and had instead organised a day at a hotel in the city. Cooper and Jenny had been in charge of all the details and Emily felt a thrill of excitement at the prospect of a relaxing day off. A whisper had spread through the office that massages were being provided for everyone, and last night Cooper had called a meeting to confirm the rumour.

"I just want to let you know some of the details for tomorrow," he began as the chatter died down in the room. "Many of you have heard that there'll be massages." Several people murmured. "A couple of people have told me quietly that they *do not* want to have a massage with their workmates." There was laughter throughout the small group. "I want to reassure you that you won't have to do anything awkward. We have a lovely day planned for you. The hotel has brought in several local businesses to pamper you, we have an awesome guest speaker, lunch will be spectacular, and there'll be prizes and fun all day." He smiled around the room and waved his hand in Jenny's direction. "Jenny has done an amazing job of organizing the details and I've squeezed Ed Simpson for all the cash he could spare." A small cheer rippled through the room and Cooper put his hands up. "One last thing. You know we have invited all of your partners to the dinner tomorrow night. For some of you this might be the only time you escape from your children for a night out. So, it's not mandatory to join in the group dinner. If you'd rather squirrel yourself away in a corner of the other restaurant on site and have a romantic dinner together, we totally understand and your meal will be covered. This is meant to be a reward, after all!" Another cheer had sounded as Cooper dismissed them and suggested they go home early.

As she'd passed him in the doorway on her way back to her office, Cooper had pulled her aside. "You don't have a significant other that you'll be dining with in the corner do you?"

"You know I don't."

"Just checking. I'd hate to get an awkward surprise tomorrow."

She batted her eyelashes and said in a whisper. "It's a bit late to ask if I'm seeing someone isn't it? You should have asked that when you first arrived— before you set your sights on me, again."

~

*A*fter speeches, awards, team building games and an enormous lunch, complete with stationery themed cupcakes, the workers from Simpsons were split into smaller groups and directed to various stores in the city. Emily didn't think it was a coincidence that she and Cooper were allocated to a boutique spa several blocks away. As they walked there together she commented as much to him. "Just the two of us going to this particular place? Very convenient for you."

He smirked and took her hand. "Oh, don't be salty. You know I'm an evil genius."

"How did you get this one past Jenny? What excuse did you use? Please don't say it's because we are management and should go somewhere separate."

His laughter filled the street. "Are you serious? This was Jenny's idea."

"I'll kill her."

"No you won't. You'll thank her—trust me."

"I don't trust you. Not one bit."

"Oh, come on, I'm completely trustworthy. I

haven't told a soul about your crime spree the other week. Not even my newest buddy Luke."

"I've watched you carefully every time we've been with him and Jordan, just to make sure."

"Really? What about last Thursday when he and I went out to play pool? Where were your spying eyes, then?" He grinned at the shocked look on her face.

"You went out with Luke? Why didn't you tell me?"

"Bro code." He said mysteriously and stopped at a pink painted door. "This is us." Soothing music played inside and the shop front smelled amazing. He approached the desk and announced their arrival to the beautifully groomed receptionist.

"Thanks for coming a few minutes early." She stood and handed them each a clipboard. "Please fill these in." She led them through a frosted door and indicated they should sit on two low chairs. "Our therapists will be with you shortly and explain your treatment. You'll be having the couple's massage last of all, today." She closed the door behind her and Emily looked at Cooper.

"Couple's massage? What the hell have you organised?"

"You'll see."

"This is a bad idea."

"No, it isn't. Fill in your form and stop worrying. You're here to be pampered."

"I kind of thought it would be in private."

"The first part is. Don't worry, you'll love it."

She pursed her lips and filled in her form as her heart beat a million miles an hour. A couple's massage was the last thing she'd expected. Keeping her clothes on around Cooper was high on her list of priorities.

Two therapists appeared, offered them water and showed them where to change. Emily scurried into the bathroom and quickly slipped into the robe she'd been supplied. Her eyes were round in the mirror and she resisted the urge for a quick pep talk before she returned to the hallway.

Stop being childish. You probably won't run into him out there anyway.

A basket had been supplied for her belongings and she carried it in front of her as she returned to the room where she'd been asked to wait. Cooper was already there and he leaned against the wall, waiting for her.

He took her basket and placed it on the ground. When he straightened up, he was way too close. His fingers tucked a strand of her hair behind her ear and he smiled his trademark surfer grin. If she hadn't already been on edge, her knees might have gone weak at the sight of that smile. Knowing he was naked under that robe wasn't helping.

"Ready?"

"As I'll ever be."

"This is your room." He pointed to a door on the

left, then leaned in close, "Just remember, our massage is last." She watched him almost skip down the hallway, whistling as he went.

Damn him. Now I'll spend the whole time thinking about what will happen once we're in there together.

An hour later she found herself in the shower, rinsing off the mud exfoliant that had been expertly applied all over her body. The shower gel had a citrus scent and she rubbed it liberally across her skin, creating bubbles as her hands moved. Eyes closed, she enjoyed the hot water cascading down her back as she washed the last of the mud away.

When she reappeared in the hallway, wrapped in a clean robe, the therapist directed her toward the couple's room.

Emily held her breath. With no idea what to expect, she allowed herself to be led into the room. A sigh escaped her lips as her fears were put to rest—the two massage tables were a good distance apart. Her visions of him holding her hand or something equally corny, fled. The giant hot tub in the corner did not escape her notice, though, and panic slithered up her spine.

Please, please, don't ask us to get in there together.

Cooper arrived next and the therapist excused herself for a few minutes. He wasted no time pulling Emily toward him. "How was it?"

"Amazing. You?"

"Really great. It's been a very long time since I've had a massage."

She bit her lip. "This is my first one."

"What? You've never had a massage before?"

"Never. I've been kind of shy about taking off my clothes."

He grinned and tipped her chin up. Their eyes met before he spoke, "You were never shy in front of me."

"That's different." Her breath caught in her throat as their thick robes touched and his warm hand caressed her cheek. "I don't know what I'm meant to do here," she whispered. His fingers tickled the wet tendrils of hair on the back of her neck and she resisted the urge to close her eyes. "You really have to stop that."

His answering groan made her smile as he took a small step back. "You're right. Ignore me. I get carried away whenever you are close."

A giggle escaped her lips. Part discomfort; part awkwardness. "Please tell me we're not getting in the hot tub."

"I wish I could say we were," he laughed as her eyes widened, "but I told them we weren't actually a couple and it would be wildly inappropriate." As the door opened and two therapists appeared he threw a sidelong glance at Emily. "Next time, though. Promise."

The blush that crept up her neck added to the warmth in the room but the staff didn't seem to notice. They set about getting their towels ready and soon indicated it was time to start. After some quick instructions to lie face down on the bed and cover themselves with the towels, they left the room again.

Emily stared at Cooper, not daring to move toward the massage table. He rolled his eyes and turned to face the wall without her having to demand it. His laughter made her feel childish as she quickly dropped the robe and covered herself with the towel. When it was his turn to lie down, she turned her face to the wall, grinding her teeth as he continued to laugh. "Why are you laughing? This is so awkward!"

"The look on your face is priceless," he said, as she listened to him settling himself on the table. "You can turn around now." She turned and groaned. The towels were pink and where she had covered her entire body with hers, he'd slung his loosely over his bottom. She kept her eyes on his face, not daring to let them glide over his naked back. A muscled back she'd once run her hands over in a hotel bed. "Did you really think I'd insist on watching?"

"I don't know what to think."

"You can relax. I've just been teasing you—we're not having a couple's massage."

"Why are we in the same room then?"

"They're going to put a divider between us, that's why the beds are so far apart. I'll be able to hear you groan if she digs her fingers into your back, but that's about it."

"I truly don't understand." She glared at him from her side of the room.

"We're at this place because there weren't enough spaces at the other ones. This room was the only one available for this last hour and I thought it would be better, rather than us cutting the afternoon short."

"You're a devil. You had me panicking!"

"Sorry." He laughed. "It was too temping not to tease you. Just like the lights in the sky, though, when you give in I'll take you for a real massage as a couple. Promise."

"No more promises from you, Cooper Jackson. Every one of them is designed to get me into trouble!"

~

*E*mily sat at her desk the next morning, finishing a few small tasks before she and Cooper interviewed for the vacant warehouse roles. She was having trouble concentrating, thinking instead of their dinner conversation the night before. Their staff, chatting and laughing with each other had surrounded them, but in between they'd laughed together, reminiscing about their few weeks together last year. Every time he took her out she ended up laughing her way through dinner with him, and last night had been no exception.

They'd talked a lot about her friends…

"I know Jordan is with Luke, but did she ever hear from the guy from the baseball game that we joined her for? I think about that day a lot."

"The bondage guy with the liquorice collar? I don't know what happened to him, but I'm really glad they didn't hit it off. I wouldn't have been able to look at her quite the same after that."

"I imagine not. He seemed to want to come home with us after she left, didn't you think?"

"At the time I did think that's what he wanted. When she rushed to her car and left us standing there I was so worried he'd want to explain why he'd made that collar and why he liked it. That was the last thing I wanted to know."

"You know he contacted me a few weeks later?"

"No way?" her eyes widened. "What for?"

"It was the strangest call. You and I had broken up by then so I didn't really want to talk to him, but he was following me up to see if I wanted to invest in some shares."

"Really? It was work related?"

"Yep. Apparently he was not remotely ashamed that we'd met while he spent the day tied to a railing with a liquorice lead. He wanted to be my broker if I ever got into trading shares."

She'd choked on her wine, wondering if Jordan knew her date had contacted her friends behind her back. As always, Cooper was full of interesting revelations and enormous belly laughs.

Her eyes refocussed on her laptop and as she snapped it closed and pulled it from the holder to take downstairs, she saw someone in a bright yellow suit walk past her door. She frowned as she stood up and went to see who it was.

She didn't recognise the person so she followed them and soon found herself in the sales section. The gentleman in question sat at a desk and started typing while Emily continued into the sales manager's office and closed the door. He took one look at her face and raised his hand.

"I'm already on it, Emily."

"How can you even know what I'm going to say?" she laughed.

"I know because you have the same look that's been on a couple of people's faces today. The same look I saw on my own face when my newest staff member, Rodney Wolf out there, showed up in his prized canary yellow zoot suit."

She laughed again and raised both her hands. "You got me. What the hell is a zoot suit, and which era does it come from?" She settled herself in his visitor chair.

"It's the thing of beauty you just witnessed, made famous in the jazz era. They're a collector's item, young Rodney informs me. I took the opportunity to inform him that those baggy pants and wide lapels were not suitable work attire, even if they are a most fetching canary yellow." He smiled at her across his desk. "He won't wear it again, I promise. He's not leaving the office today so none of our customers will have to endure the sight either."

"That's great Liam. Thanks for taking care of it before I even found out."

"It's a shame you didn't see him earlier to get the full effect." He smirked as she got up to leave. "He was wearing a matching yellow wide brimmed hat with a feather in it. I think he thinks he's the guy from The Mask."

⁓

"Cooper?" Emily called as she rounded the corner of his office. "Are you ready?"

His head poked up from under the desk. "I'm ready. Why are we doing this downstairs again?"

"I thought the guys coming for these interviews might feel a bit more comfortable in the small office downstairs." She stood back as he pulled his computer cord from under the desk. "Going somewhere?"

"I'm just bringing my charger. Someone booked eight interviews on one day and my laptop won't make it to the end." He eyed her meaningfully and she grinned back at him.

"These will be shorter than the others, I promise. Anyway, we got out of doing the sales interviews now that we promoted Liam to the sales manager role. You should be happy about that. Sales people can be odd."

"I'm happy about one aspect of that—the part where you delegated sitting in on those interviews to Jenny."

They fell into step as they walked down the corridor toward the stairs. "Jenny is more than capable—she would have been with me if you hadn't insisted you were spending every day of the last few weeks shadowing me."

When they reached the conference room Sasha had already settled their first applicant at the table. Emily chuckled to herself as she heard a sharp intake of breath beside her. Clearly Cooper didn't realise what he was in for.

"Hi there Noel."

"Hello." He shook both their hands and Cooper tried his best to hide his surprise. Noel was wearing a death metal t-shirt with a profanity printed in big red letters on the back. His greasy hair hung in thick sections around his face, hiding his pale skin. As they questioned him, he explained his background was as a welder and that he hadn't been able to find work in his own field. Emily thought he had promise, but Cooper marked him a big no on his score sheet.

Their next applicant arrived in blue jeans and sneakers, with headphones dangling around his neck. He introduced himself as Jay, even though his resume listed his name as Thomas.

"What would you bring to this role?" Cooper asked and once again, Emily could tell by the tone of his voice that he was unimpressed.

"Well, I'm friendly.

"How much warehouse experience have you had?"

"Well, I haven't worked in an actual warehouse. But I've taken care of the equipment for my band for a while now, which is kind of similar. You have to keep track of all the boxes and make sure everything is sent at your end, and received at the other end. I use a forklift to unload our bigger speakers but I don't have my licence yet." Cooper twitched beside her. "I probably can't start for a month either, so I hope that's okay."

"You need to give a month's notice to your employer?" Emily made a note on his resume.

"Nah, we're touring with the band. We leave tonight and we'll be back next month. I can start as soon as I get back, as long as we don't get extended." He grinned. "You know, if we're successful."

"Well, I think that's all we need for now." Cooper was quick to end the interview. "We'll be in touch."

When the door closed behind him Cooper blew out a long breath. "This is awful. I can't believe people come to job interviews in jeans!"

"It's pretty normal for warehouse or trade roles. They just don't seem to dress up. The next guy was

137

recommended by one of our current staff so fingers crossed he's decent."

Finger crossing didn't help. The recommended applicant slouched in his chair and barely made eye contact. He grunted a few answers and looked around the room, like he had somewhere else to be. When he asked if he could have a break to get a cigarette after just five minutes with them, they told him they'd let him know.

And that's how their day proceeded. Eight men, in attire that varied from high visibility work gear to jeans and hoodies made it through the conference room.

One of them tracked dirt from his workbooks right through the building, and another left his lunch box behind and had to return to pick it up. When he opened the door and they were interviewing someone else he reached in and grabbed his item without a word of apology.

The last applicant was a lot chattier than the rest and Emily and Cooper finally got some answers to their many questions. Greg Garrett was nothing, if not honest, when Emily asked him why he would be a good fit.

"I've only had two back injuries in the two years I've been working in my current job, so that's good, right?"

"I guess." Cooper's tone said he didn't quite

agree. "How do you get along with the other staff at your current position?"

"I'm friends with everyone, except for this one guy. I'm not sure if he's a bit crazy or if he just hates me, but at least once a month he reports me to management for something I haven't done. Last month it was taking paper home from the stationery room. The month before he said I messed with the time clock. Another time he said I ate part of his lunch. I wasn't even at work that day. I think he's just evil."

"That sounds like a hard situation to deal with. How are you managing?"

"Well, I'm not, which is why I'm looking for a new job. At my going away lunch I intend to punch that guy in the mouth."

~

"*I*s it too late to change my mind and stop sitting in on interviews?"

"You big baby. We only have the ones you actually should be sitting in on to go. Operations manager and accounts manager both require your input, but not today. I'm done." Emily slouched in her chair while Cooper leaned against her doorframe.

"Big plans for the weekend?"

"Not really. Dinner tonight at Luke's house, then

I'll be trying to clear my inbox of some of the backlog. I have to pack for my trip next week, too."

"Sounds like you'll be busy." He sounded wistful and she looked up to find him staring straight at her. His eyes raked over her face and for a moment a look of longing settled on his features, but it was quickly washed away and he shook himself with a short laugh. "I'm tired too. I guess I'll think about going home." He pushed away from the door and she suddenly couldn't take it any more.

"Cooper," she called as he turned away. "Do you want to come to Luke's?"

"Would I be welcome?"

"Of course. You and Luke have the bro code, remember? Everyone likes you."

"I wasn't talking about everyone." He stepped back into the room and closed the door behind him. "I'm talking specifically about you, Emily. Do you want me to come tonight?"

She hesitated for a moment, knowing that an honest answer could set her up for heartbreak all over again. A dishonest answer, however, would leave her wondering what might have been. Better to have tried and lost, than to have never tried at all. She was tired of keeping him at arm's length. "Yes, I want you to come."

"Why?"

"Does there have to be a reason?"

"Usually." He watched her from the doorway, his blue eyes missing nothing.

"I don't have a reason, Cooper. I enjoyed your company last time, I know Luke likes you and that's all the explanation I can offer you right now."

"I guess that will have to do. For now." He searched her face again, satisfied with her answer. "Text me the address?"

"How about I just take you with me? How long until you can leave?"

"Ten minutes or so."

"Okay. Come get me when you're ready. I brought a change of clothes so I could go straight there. We'll swing by your hotel and then we'll go together."

CHAPTER 13

What are you thinking, Emily? You're playing with fire. Spending time socially with Cooper is a bad idea.

It might be a bad idea, but it was a deliciously bad idea. Emily quickly changed in Cooper's bathroom while he got dressed in his room. For a fleeting second the idea that they were both naked in the same suite entered her head but she swiftly sent that thought on its way. This was just a convenient way to save driving back and forth before going to Luke's for dinner. Nothing more.

She touched up her make up and gave her hair a quick brush, tying it up in a long swinging ponytail. When she'd shoved her work clothes back into her bag she waited in the tiny kitchen for Cooper.

He appeared two minutes later, clean-shaven and smelling of a familiar woody scent—the one that caught her attention in the coffee shop where they first met. "Just need my shoes and I'm ready. Do we need to stop and get a bottle of wine or something?"

"Nope. Luke said he'd take care of everything since it was a workday. He's a good guy."

"Right, let's go then."

She followed him out to the elevator, sneaking quick peaks at his shoulders or his face whenever he wasn't looking at her. She'd always loved running her hand along his cheek when he was clean-shaven and her hand itched to do it now.

What is wrong with me? Why do I have butterflies in my stomach like a schoolgirl?

She worried to herself in the elevator. Tonight was going to test her resolve to stay away from Cooper.

~

"Hey, isn't that the guy who was skydiving with us, Luke?" Jordan pointed at the television they were watching in the lounge room. Dinner had left them stuffed and they'd spread out on Luke's leather couches to recover, with Jordan's dog, Rex, watching them intently from the floor.

"That's him. Looks like he's hit the big time if he's getting his own show. Did you know him and that girl are together?"

"No way? They actually got together? How do you know?"

"She had her car serviced at work a few months later and we got chatting. Rachel, her name is."

Jordan ran her fingers through the back of his hair. "I had to search all year to find you and she just had to go skydiving one time. That is mightily unfair."

"Well, in her defence I was there almost from the start. You just wouldn't *see* me."

"True. I'm glad you made me."

"Me too." He leaned close and kissed her and the others started cheering and teasing. They broke apart, laughing, as Jordan snuggled into this shoulder. "You guys are just jealous!" he called out to them as Shelly and Boyd snuggled on another lounge. At the sound of Luke's raised voice, Rex raised his head from floor next to their feet. He sniffed the air and then settled down again, satisfied that all was well.

"There's so much love in this room, I can barely stand it. Andrea, you should have brought Lori then you could have joined in, too!"

"She's working, otherwise we'd be here showing you how loved up we are, trust me. Maybe next time we can have dinner on a weekend when she's not working."

"She works in a restaurant, right?"

"Yep. The only night she gets off is Sunday. It sucks."

"I'll keep that in mind next time we invite you to our humble abode."

"Well, on that note, I'm going home." Emily

stood from the chair where she'd been stretched out. "There's way too much romance in here for me." She made a face at Jordan and then waved her hand at Cooper. "Are you ready?"

"You're driving, and I am your adoring passenger, so I'm ready when you say I'm ready."

His words set off another round of laughter and Emily shook her head as she waved goodbye to her friends. She didn't miss Luke making kissing faces at her on the way out. Cooper was slipping on his shoes, which stopped him from seeing the teasing she had to endure.

They walked down the stairs of Luke's house and crunched their way down the long gravel driveway to the street. As they walked Cooper slipped his hand into hers.

"What are you doing?"

"Holding my friend's hand. I wouldn't want you to fall on the uneven gravel." He grinned to himself, not making eye contact but staring at the ground.

"I'm a big girl Cooper."

"So you keep reminding me." He gave her hand a small squeeze and grinned to himself some more. "You didn't pull away. You want to hold my hand too. That room full of emotion has slithered past your defences."

"Not necessarily. Maybe I just don't want to fall."

They both laughed as they reached the car and Cooper finally freed her fingers. He wasn't done with her, though, and he gently leaned her against the car, moving so that his body covered hers.

His hand slipped into the back of her hair and it was exactly what she'd missed all these months. The way he twisted his fingers and tugged the strands just a little filled her with nostalgia for their first kiss. His eyes bored into hers as the smell of him up close filled her senses and the familiar feel of him quickly intoxicated her. For almost two months she'd resisted his pull. Reminded herself that they were work colleagues and that he had no place in her life anymore. She was so wrong. There was nowhere else he belonged than with her. Nine months apart had convinced her of that, no matter what she'd said to her naughty bird in her most unhappy moments.

"Cooper—"

"Shhhh..." his lips brushed against hers and she closed her eyes. A small sigh escaped and he smiled as he dropped tiny kisses on the corner of her mouth. "I've wanted to do that from the first Tuesday I wandered into your office."

She looked up into his eyes, still fixed on hers. They looked darker out here by the car. Dark and smouldering eyes were the last things she needed to add to the list of attractive traits that Cooper possessed.

"This is a bad idea."

"Only because we work together. For every other reason it is a spectacularly good idea." He ran his finger across her cheek. "I've missed you. More than I thought possible."

She closed her eyes again, trying to block out those magnetising eyes. All she wanted was to give in and be with him. Spend her nights snuggled up in his arms. Talk about everything they'd missed together since she'd stopped taking his calls. Even tell him the mistaken reason that had happened. He nuzzled her hair and set goose bumps skittering over her flesh, and she realised he didn't much feel like talking tonight.

Her hands gripped his forearms and she gently pulled his hands away from her hair. "I cannot think straight when you do that." She chuckled and he wrapped his hands around her waist instead.

"Better?"

"A little. Come on, let's go before we have an audience and I have to field calls from every one of them all weekend."

"I like that your friends are so invested in your love life. I feel like Luke is totally rooting for me." He grinned and moved to the passenger side of the car. "Usually men are in competition, but I've practically got a voluntary wing man."

"Oh, you noticed he always make sure we sit together, did you? I'm going to kick his ass when I see him next!"

"I noticed, and I like it."

Emily started the car and pointed them in the

direction of his hotel. All her senses were on high alert. She was short of breath as her insides twisted, and she argued with herself all the way over what she should do.

She should go straight home as soon as he was safely out of the car. She knew that like she knew her own address. To make sure it happened, she pulled up outside his door and left the car running.

"You need to come upstairs."

"It's not a good idea, Cooper."

He sighed and undid his seatbelt, then he turned to her with a new light in his eyes. "You left your clothes upstairs."

"Damn! I actually need those to take away with me on Monday."

He grinned and slipped out of the car before bending down and leaning in. "Guess you're coming up then."

She scowled and switched off the ignition.

How am I going to resist him once we're behind closed doors? No way is he going to hand me my clothes and wave goodbye.

As they waited for the elevator Cooper took her hand again and she turned wide eyes on him. "What?"

"Bad idea." His finger rubbed over the back of her hand and then started to make circular movements. "Very bad idea," she muttered to herself as the door opened and he pulled her inside. Once the door closed she was lost.

He pulled her hard against him and wrapped his arms around her, trapping her arms under his. He waited a moment, making sure she didn't object, before his lips descended on hers, the warmth of his lips making her insides somersault.

Pull away. Stop this now. Don't let yourself step into that hotel room!

He tugged her along the hallway, as a small smile played around his lips. He looked like a man with a plan and Emily's legs wobbled at the thought that it obviously included her.

Who am I kidding? I don't want to be anywhere else.

As he unlocked the door and indicated she should go before him she had a moment where she could have stopped what was about to happen. Could have said 'thanks, but no, I'll just get my clothes and be on my merry way'. Could have insisted on staying outside the door until he returned with her belongings.

Instead, she strode through the door and dropped her keys onto the kitchen bench.

The moment she turned, he was upon her, drinking her in, his mouth exploring hers with an urgent need. He captured her ponytail, twisting it around his fingers, and she gasped as his other hand clutched at her waist; fingers kneading her flesh, creeping down over her buttock.

She returned his need with a good dose of her own. Fingers, which had longed to touch him for weeks now had free reign to explore. She pulled his shirt out of his jeans and slipped her hands inside, feeling her way across his chest, seeking out his warmth, and pulling his own gasp from his lips. Her whole body reacted to being so close to him and small sounds of need gurgled in her throat. His hands were all over her, exploring, seeking and she let them roam wherever he wanted.

His ran his hands over her bottom as he whispered in her ear. "Promise you'll stay all night."

"I promise," she whispered, as he rained kisses across her neck.

Her words set him in motion and he bent his knees and picked her up. She wrapped her legs around his waist, her lips finding his as his tongue explored her mouth. Her arms wrapped around his neck and he turned and wobbled toward the bedroom. She pulled away from his mouth and tucked herself against him as he walked down the hall, pushing the door open with his shoulder. Excitement coursed through her veins, knowing she'd still be here tomorrow. Knowing they'd be together all weekend if she had her way.

"I hope you're ready Emily." His voice caressed her name. "I have almost a year of pent up energy to expend on you."

*E*mily didn't return home until Sunday night. As she walked through the door, a big smile on her face, Andrew let her know her absence had been unacceptable.

"Andrew's a good boy!"

She went straight to his cage to get him out. "Yes, Andrew you're a good boy. How have you been, buddy?"

His voice lowered and he dipped his feathered head, "Loooonnnneeellllllly," he said.

Emily laughed and shook her head as she set about getting him clean water and fresh seed. "How do you know what to say at just the right time? It's amazing." She muttered as she cut a piece of apple and handed it to him. He sat on top of his cage and happily ate the apple as she cleaned. "I've had a great weekend, Andrew. Cooper was a good boy."

"Coooopperrrr is naughty," he said as he continued eating his apple. "Cooooperrrr is gone."

"No, Andrew. It's time to learn some new words. Cooper is back."

"Cooper isn't coming back!"

"Yes, yes, he is. Cooper is back." She scratched his head and he leaned sideways, still holding his apple in his claw. "Can you say Cooper is back?"

"Cooper is banned from this house!"

She laughed and gave up. "Okay, I can see I brainwashed you pretty good. Poor Cooper. You're going to make his life a misery." She carried her bag to the laundry and set a load of washing going before she headed for the shower. Just a quick shower, she told herself. The last thing she needed was to get caught up in daydreaming about Cooper and what they'd done in his bathroom. Her flight was at six in the morning and she needed to pack and spend some time checking over the details of the meeting she'd be attending. She was about to travel five hours each way for a half-day meeting. To make the trip more worthwhile, she planned a stopover at their Mildura branch on the way back.

She'd be home so soon that Andrew didn't need to stay with anyone else. Jordan had offered to stick her head in for five minutes on Monday afternoon and make sure he was okay, but besides that he would be fine on his own until she returned.

Cooper had wanted to steal her away for the entire day but she'd insisted on coming home. The more time she spent with him, the more it felt like she'd never be able to leave. Being with him again was like trying on your favourite pair of gloves that had been hiding in the back of the closet. He was comfortable, and they fit.

CHAPTER 14

The early flight and the meeting passed without incident and before she knew it Emily was sitting back at the airport, waiting for the return journey. The charging cord for her phone had disappeared somewhere between the meeting and her hotel room and now her battery was running low. Her laptop was fully charged, however, so she could still get some work done and she smiled as she deleted three cute emails Cooper had sent her. His businesslike persona had disappeared the moment her head had dropped onto his pillow.

Her flight would be called in twenty minutes and for a second she considered buying a new charging cable from one of the many airport stores. There were three perfectly good ones at home in a drawer, though, and she didn't need another. There was no reason she'd need her phone on the plane and she planned to take an airport taxi to the office when she landed. She shrugged and tucked it away in her handbag. Charging could wait until she got to the Mildura office and borrowed someone's charger.

Her flight was announced and she boarded, smiling at the two stewards as they welcomed her aboard. Settled in her seat, she decided not to work, but to read her book instead—something she hadn't had time to do in many, many months. A smile played around her lips as she lost herself in the words.

This was how air travel should be every time.

～

*A*s Cooper passed Emily's office, her phone was ringing. He'd heard it ring once or twice already and now it occurred to him that it could only be a direct call. Sasha would have taken a message if it had gone through the main switch.

He walked across the room and picked up the phone. "Simpsons Stationery, Emily Pennington's phone."

"Can I speak to Emily please? It's urgent."

"I'm afraid she's out of the office until tomorrow. Can I take a message for you, or could somebody else help?"

"Cooper, is that you?"

"Yes, who is this?"

"It's Jordan. I've been trying to get Emily on her

mobile but she's not answering. She must be in the air."

He glanced at his watch. "Yes, she won't land for hours yet. You said it was urgent, what's wrong?"

"There was a fire in her block of units."

"Oh shit. Is it bad?"

"Yeah. There's not much left. I'm her emergency contact so the landlord called me an hour ago."

"Jesus." He ran his fingers through his hair. Emily would be devastated when she found out. He'd seen how house proud she was, always adding touches here and there to make her feel more at home.

"Do you have a number for wherever she was going?"

"I do, hang on." He flicked through a folder on her desk and then his hand stilled. "Jordan, what about Andrew?"

"You won't believe it but it was Andrew who raised the alarm. They would have lost a lot more of the building if someone hadn't heard him screaming out for help. They managed to break the door down and save him. Apparently the neighbours thought it was a person calling out."

Cooper snickered. "I shouldn't laugh, but that sounds like Andrew."

"Yeah. They told me he was actually screaming, 'Help! Help!' at the top of his lungs."

Cooper laughed outright then. "Well, I'm glad he's okay. I can't find the damn number for the

Mildura office, Jordan, I'll have to come back to you."

"Okay, if you could call me back, that'd be great. Andrew lost a few feathers and he's been very quiet so I need to talk to her to know what to do."

"Do you think he'd be okay to travel in the car?"

"I can't see why not. Why?"

"I'm seriously considering driving up to the office and telling her in person. I'd take the bird so she can see first hand that he's okay. I'm going to guess he's pretty stressed and maybe seeing her would be best for him."

Jordan giggled to herself and Cooper rolled his eyes before she spoke. "That's a really nice thing to do. You've got it bad for her, haven't you?"

"You got me." He laughed. "I'll give you my number. If you can text me your address I'll come and get him and then I'll leave straight away. Can you stop trying her phone? If she lands and has twenty missed calls she'll freak out."

"She's a big girl, Cooper. She'll handle this. It's just stuff she's lost, it can all be replaced."

"I know. I just don't want her to have to handle the news alone."

~

*F*ive hours in the car with Andrew turned out to be the worst idea Cooper had ever had. The bird had been droopy when he'd picked him up, but he'd gone to the pet store and bought new seed and a special container that wouldn't spill his water in the car. After a few minutes of eating quietly in the corner of his cage, he'd walked across the perch and looked sideways at Cooper.

"How are you doing, mate? Your wing looks a bit funny where you lost those feathers. Emily will know what to do with you."

"Coooooooperrrrrrrr."

"Yes. That's me. Please don't start being mean like you were in the office."

The bird looked at him and walked sideways along his perch, back toward his food. "Coooooooperrrrrrrr is naughty."

"Oh, here we go." He kept his eyes on the road as the parrot rattled off all his phrases again.

"Coooooooperrrrrrrr smells."

"Thanks."

"Coooooooperrrrrrrr is banned from this house."

"Okay."

"Coooooooperrrrrrrr is poop!"

"Wow. She was really angry with me, wasn't she, mate?"

"We'll burn the bed! Coooooooperrrrrrrr can't sing."

"I can sing. Listen." He turned the radio up and started singing along with the song that played. He glanced at Andrew every so often and the bird stared at him as he belted out the words. Several songs played one after the other and Cooper sang and sang, happy to see he'd found something to silence his accuser. When the news came on he turned the volume down and addressed a now-silent Andrew. "How'd you like that?"

"Andrew can siiiiiing."

"So can I. I just proved it."

Andrew turned his back and leaned toward his seed. In a low tone, almost to himself he said. "Coooooooperrrrrrrrr sucks."

~

"You ou drove all this way to give me the news in person?"

"I did. I figured you'd try to get home straight away. This way I can drive you and you don't have to worry about anything."

She nodded, lost in her thoughts. "Did Jordan say how much damage?"

"She said it was pretty bad. Andrew saved the day, though."

That news finally made Emily smile and she tickled Andrew under the chin. He was perched on her finger as they made their way home. His made a clicking sound with his tongue and rolled his head so she could scratch him in his favourite place.

"I'm so glad you're okay." She said to him as she kissed him on his head. "Your feathers will grow back like new."

"Coooooooperrrrrrrr smells."

She laughed and Cooper frowned as he drove. "Don't encourage him. He's abused me the whole way here. At one point I considered setting him free, he was so annoying. He liked my singing though. That shut him up for a good seven minutes at a stretch, didn't it Andrew."

The bird eyed him and snuggled closer to Emily. "Coooooooperrrrrrrr."

"That's me buddy."

"Coooooooperrrrrrrr."

"Yep, what you got? Some new insult to hurl at me? I think I've heard them all by now."

Cooper grinned and Andrew crawled up on to Emily's shoulder. He flapped his good wing and made his clicking sounds. Emily looked out the window until the bird started flapping crazily on her shoulder. She put him on her hand and then leaned across and put him back in his cage. He climbed up onto his perch and started up his screaming at Cooper again. It was so loud they couldn't hear themselves think as he repeated over and over all the ways that Cooper had wronged them.

"Stop the car."

"What? Why?" Cooper pulled the car over as soon as he could find room.

"Because I can't stand the screaming."

"Don't do anything drastic, Emily."

She laughed. "Oh get off, I'm not going to let him loose, idiot." She pulled a towel from her suitcase and opened the back door. Andrew saw what was coming and he shouted louder and faster while she moved the towel toward him. As she threw it over the cage he shrieked, "She loves me best!" and then he was silent.

Emily got back in the front and they continued toward home. Cooper frowned and looked over at her, as she sat staring out the window, lost again in thoughts of her damaged house.

He spoke into the blissful silence. "That towel would have come in mighty handy six hours ago."

❦

*E*mily's unit was unliveable. The insurance assessor declared the building still structurally sound, but the repairs would take many months to complete. Simpsons promised a sizeable donation to help her get back on her feet and Cooper convinced her to stay with him for a night or two, until she could decide where she was going to live.

Andrew seemed to sense that Emily was upset and he behaved himself for once. The hotel advised that if they received any complaints he would have to go, but they were prepared to have him if he could be quiet, once Cooper explained the situation.

Emily went through the next days as though she was in a trance. She went to work and still gave her all, handling the workload like the professional she was, but at night she fell into bed, too exhausted to eat or even talk. Cooper held her close and she slept soundly beside him.

When Saturday rolled around she was wide awake at six. Cooper snored softly beside her and she tiptoed to the kitchen to make herself a coffee. Andrew's cage was covered and he remained silent while she sat at the kitchen table. She sipped her coffee and scrolled through the news on her phone, feeling better than she had all week. Cooper's phone vibrated in the charger and she leaned over to look at the screen.

The phone buzzed and the word MUM appeared on the screen.

What? His Mum?

Glancing over her shoulder, she disconnected the phone and quietly answered, "Hello?"

"Hello can I speak to Cooper please?" a husky female voice asked. She let out a racking cough and then asked. "Who is this?"

"This is Emily. Who is this?"

"Oooh, a girlfriend. I never get to speak to them." She giggled, "I'm Cooper's mother, dear. But he never comes to visit me. Always says he loves me and he'll visit but never does. I think he's ashamed of his old mum, I do. Is he there? Or is he avoiding me again?"

Emily closed her eyes as her pulse slammed in her ears.

That lying bastard. He told me his mother was dead!

"Cooper is out at the moment. Do you want to call back in about an hour or so?"

"I can try. They don't always let me near the phone here. Can you tell him I called?"

"I'll write him a message." She promised through gritted teeth before disconnecting the call.

She wanted to wake him up and demand an answer. Scream and yell and accuse him of everything all over again. Dread settled in the pit of her stomach as she recognised the misery sweeping over her. Exactly like last time. She'd thought it was another woman back then, only to discover it was his mother. Now the same mother, the one he'd told her was dead, was going to come between them again.

It didn't matter that he wasn't seeing someone else. He'd lied to her—straight to her face. In some ways it was worse than last time; at least she hadn't given him a chance to explain back then.

She wouldn't now, either. She was done with Cooper Jackson. Her bag sat by the couch and she shoved as many of her clothes into it as she could find. Bathroom items were retrieved as quietly as possible and she threw them in on top of the clothes.

She slipped her shoes on, packed up her phone and her work computer, and dragged the heavy bags over her shoulder. There weren't enough of her clothes left after the fire to justify leaving some of them in his bedroom but there was no way she would risk waking him to retrieve them.

She picked up Andrew's cage, murmuring to him to please stay quiet under his blanket, and for once, he obeyed. When she was safely into the lift she pulled off the blanket and he looked her straight in the eye as she fought not to cry. He rubbed his head against the cage and she put her face down near him. True to form he made his feelings known. "Coooooooperrrrrrrr's dead!"

CHAPTER 15

"*I*f you want the role, Emily, it's yours." Ed sat back in his chair, a big smile on his face. He was obviously pleased with himself.

"Wow. I don't know what to say. It's an unexpected surprise."

"You don't have to give me an answer right now. Sleep on it and let me know tomorrow. Cooper left an extensive list of decent applicants who would be great as our new operations manager if you decide to turn it down. We're happy for you to stay as human resources manager if that's where your heart truly lies."

My heart lies with the man I've spent the last three months working beside.

"I don't need to sleep on it, I'll take it. You're right that I've been doing the work anyway. It's been busy and the hours have been long but I've enjoyed the variety and the chance to learn so much about the whole business. I'm looking forward to taking some of the improvements we decided on to fruition."

"Perfect! I'm glad. Your first job is to replace yourself. I know Cooper isn't here to interview with you but you can choose a suitable replacement. It could be the last interview you have time to sit in on once you're in charge."

"It's not an issue. I have someone in mind already."

Ed stood up and shook her hand. Instead of leaving her office, he leaned against the desk and folded his arms. "I promised myself I wasn't going to interfere, and I'm sure you know what's best for you, but I can't help myself. I hope you'll give Cooper another chance, Emily."

"Thanks Ed. I appreciate your concern. I don't know what to think about Cooper at the moment and I'm annoyed with myself for letting down my guard. That's not something you have to worry about with me again. I will never again date someone I'm working with."

"Oh, it's not so bad. Sometimes us workaholics have nowhere else to meet people, besides at the office." He grinned at her and picked up his briefcase. "Either way, think about it before you decide you two are done for good. I've known Cooper for a long time and I've never seen him as down as he is now. I'm sharing a confidence when I say that he pretty much thought you were the one."

"It's highly unprofessional for him to have told you that." She ground her teeth together.

What was he thinking saying that to the man I work for?

"It was off the record. Said in a completely private setting. We're friends outside of work, you know."

"I didn't know that, but thanks for making me feel better."

"Well, I'm off. Got a long drive back home." He turned at the door, "Think about what I said. You could do a lot worse than my friend Cooper." He smiled and was gone.

I could kill your friend Cooper, right now!

~

She came out of the building at the end of the day to find Cooper sitting on the bonnet of her car in the dark. She stopped and watched him, before he could look up and see her. His chin was in one hand as his fingers moved over his phone screen. For a second she considered turning back, but she owed him an enormous thank you and now was as good a time as any to deliver it. In fact, it could be her only chance. She wasn't likely to see him again after today.

She was still angry with him, though, and she couldn't help but take an aggressive approach. "My note gave you specific instructions Cooper. I don't want to see you." Emily stepped around him and put her laptop on the passenger seat.

He slid off the bonnet and waited for her to return to the driver's side. "I got the instructions. It's not every day you have the best weekend of your life and wake to find a note that reads 'Your dead mother called. <u>Do</u> <u>Not</u> Contact Me!!!! Complete with capitals, underlines and exclamation points."

"Well, it's not every day you answer the phone to discover your boyfr—" she paused, "that *people* have lied and other people are not dead." She walked past him, intent on getting in the car and driving off. Curiosity got the better of her, though, and she turned back toward him. If they were to go their separate ways, she had to know why he'd been so dishonest. "Why did you tell me she was dead, Cooper?"

"Can I take you to dinner and explain?"

"No."

"Right, well it's a long drawn-out tale." He glanced at the darkened office. "Has everyone left?"

"Yes. I'm the last one here. Why?"

"Because it's private. I'm not in the habit of talking about my mother."

"You sure talked about her a lot the day the photo frame broke."

He grimaced. "I'm so sorry about that. You put

170

me on the spot and I started babbling and I couldn't stop. Like I said, I rarely discuss her."

"You carry her photo around."

"No, I don't. I had her photo with me because I was trying to psyche myself up to go and visit her. I wanted to convince myself that she wasn't so bad."

"What could be so bad about her that you tell people she's dead?" She should get in the car and go, but she wanted to hear his explanation. Twice now, she'd cried over him and whatever secret he kept about his mother.

"My mother and I have never been close. I stayed away from home whenever I could, and after school I didn't come home until late. She never cared where I was, didn't even make sure that I'd eaten. When I needed school supplies she let me go without, until an aunt started buying my school gear for me each year.

"She had a job with a real estate agent and she somehow managed to embezzle a large amount of money from the business over a period of years. I don't know what she did with it all; I never saw any sign of it. Anyway, the owner of the business found out and threatened her. He said he was going to the police and he would make sure she went to jail. There was a struggle and she killed him with a knife from the office kitchen. She was convicted of murder and went to prison for fifteen years. I lived with my aunt for the last two years of high school."

Emily stared at him as he continued the story.

"She got out of prison when I was twenty eight, somehow got another job, and her boss miraculously disappeared a few months later. She's currently serving a twenty year sentence for his murder."

"She killed him too?"

"We don't know. She said she didn't do it and no body has ever been recovered. She was found guilty of his murder, though, and the court declared her mentally unsound. She was arrested driving around in his car."

"God, that's awful."

"I've had relationships break up because I told them about my mother. One woman had a relative who had been murdered and she wanted nothing to do with me after I told her. My mum has taken to calling me and texting me over and over. I ignore it mostly but occasionally I speak to her and say all the things she wants to hear. I have no intention of visiting her or of having her in my life. I didn't want to tell anyone about her. Ever."

"You could have told me."

"I probably would have, down the track. A long way down the track. Look what's happened because of her, though. Another break up because of what she's done."

"Actually it's a break up because you lied to me. You can't blame her for this."

"Indirectly it's her fault."

"Kind of. If you hadn't lied, it wouldn't have

happened, regardless of how she has behaved." She bit her lip. Now was the time to tell him about last year. "I broke up with you last time because I overheard you on a call to her." The words spilled out quickly. "I thought you were seeing someone else."

"Ahhhh... so that's what happened." A look of understanding settled on his features. "Makes sense." His tone was bitter.

"You told me it was a work call when I'd clearly heard you tell someone you loved them and would be with them soon. The next day you told me you were sending work texts but you obviously were up to something else. I decided enough was enough and I would end it before I got hurt." Cooper closed his eyes for a moment. His face was sad and she felt sorry that he'd had to carry this burden since he was a teenager.

"How can your mother even text you from prison?"

"She got hold of someone's contraband phone. Don't ask me how they get those things into the prison or what she might have done to get her hands on it. I tell myself she bribed someone."

"Can you get in trouble for communicating with her like that?

"Probably, except," he stared at the ground before answering, "I called and told them she had it."

"Wow."

"Yep. I dobbed my own mother in. Makes me a

great guy, huh?" He looked up at her, before looking away again.

"Cooper does Ed know about this?"

"Nope. Not even Ed. Imagine how clients would react to the news? They give me access to all facets of their business when I'm implementing an improvement program. Knowing someone in my family managed to embezzle funds and then committed murder to try to cover it up is probably not the best business endorsement for someone like me."

"You're not your mother." She longed to touch him. Take him in her arms and kiss his worries away. But just as he wasn't his mother, she wasn't his mother, either. This was something he would have to face up to on his own.

"I don't want to talk about my mother anymore. Can we talk about us?"

"What about us?"

"Is there still an us?" His question was hopeful, as he searched her face in the growing darkness. "Can you forgive me for telling that lie?"

"I don't know."

"That's fair enough." He slumped against the car. "I really fucked this up."

"I just need some time to digest everything that's happened." He nodded as she kept talking. "A lot of things haven't gone to plan for me. I didn't want anyone to know about you and I, but now the whole office does, including my boss. I thought we would get the staff sorted and I'd go back to enjoying my little piece of the human resources world. Now I'm the operations manager, and I don't want the staff thinking I got the job because of you and me." She shook her head and opened the car door before leaning against it. "There's a lot to consider. I need to sort out my apartment, too, and I just don't have any more space for drama right now. I'm all mixed up and I don't know how I feel. So give me some time, okay?"

He searched her face for some clue over which way she might lean. "Will you call me when you've made a decision?"

"Maybe."

"That doesn't fill me with confidence." He frowned and stepped back.

"It's all I can tell you right now, Cooper. You can't expect anything else." With those final words, she got in her car and drove slowly up the street. She didn't look back, didn't wonder what he would do now. She drove slowly as the tears coursing down her cheeks obstructed her vision.

~

"Hey Emily, are you free tonight?"

"I'm still at work, what did you have in mind?"

"I thought maybe a dinner, just you, me and Shelly? Andrea can't make it."

"Is everything okay, Jordan?"

"Yep, it's perfect, I just felt like a night out."

"Well, it's six o'clock now. I still have about half an hour before I could possibly leave and someone here will have to close up the office. Do you want to meet somewhere?"

"How about the pub?"

"I'm fine with that. It's Friday night, though, we might see Fish."

"Ha! I'm fine with Fish. He and I made our peace many months ago. I'm not about to leave Luke for the DJ!"

"As long as we've sorted that out, I'm game. I'll meet you there at half past seven."

"Awesome! I can't wait!" there was a pause as though she'd hung up. "Oh, Emily."

"Yes?"

"Wear your dancing shoes!"

∼

*A*t seven thirty Emily slipped into the booth where Shelly and Jordan were laughing hysterically together. They wiped their eyes and Shelly went to the bar to buy them a round of drinks. When she returned Jordan suggested a toast.

"To us girls, who've really managed to get our

shit together in the last year!" They all took a sip and raised another toast to the absent Andrea.

"Why couldn't she come, anyway? It's Friday night. This used to be our favourite place on Fridays."

"Something to do with Lori. She didn't say and I didn't have time to grill her. She didn't seem unhappy though." Shelly watched the people on the dance floor and a new song started.

"They seem to be going great."

"Yep. Hence my toast to us for getting our shit together!" They laughed and clinked their glasses together. "As soon as we're finished these we're dancing."

"I see Fish is popular tonight." Emily and Jordan turned in their seat to see where she was pointing. The DJ booth had been moved since they were last here and Fish was in his element leaning over the dance floor. No longer was he up in the darkened box— tonight he presided over the throng of people, just a few feet above their heads, where several of the women were close enough to call out his name. "Can't believe you didn't bag him, Jordan." She laughed as Jordan frowned at her.

"Honestly, I was spoiled for choice, remember? Fish was just one of my many admirers. How did I ever get through that year of dating?" she took a sip of her drink and looked at her friends. "I'm so glad Luke made me see reason."

"We are, too. We love him." Shelly choked on her

drink and quickly wiped her chin before she lowered her voice. "You won't believe it, there's George!" Emily turned again, and sure enough there was Shelly's cousin George. "I'm going to get him. He owes us something." She slid out of her seat, leaving the others starting after her.

"What's she talking about? What does George owe us?" Emily was mystified.

"He doesn't owe *me* anything. Maybe an apology for nearly getting me killed." Jordan's face showed distaste at the thought of the one night she'd been on a date with George last year. "Why couldn't Shelly just pretend she didn't see him?"

"No idea, but they're coming this way." Emily gave her a sympathetic stare as they slid over to make room for the others.

"Oh! Hello Jordan." George frowned and turned to Shelly. "Shelly, we can catch up another time."

"No way!" She grabbed his arm and forced him into the booth. "I have questions for you and the only time I see you these days is when the family is around. You are my prisoner!" She laughed and shoved him forward so he was sitting opposite Jordan.

"What's so important that you have to know the details right now?" he put his beer on the table and glared at Shelly.

"I want to know," she stopped and cleared her throat. "Correction. We all want to know what the hell you were thinking the night you took Jordan to

McDonalds and then to that underground-illegal-maybe-we-might-die-here garage." Jordan gasped as her words sank in and Emily's eyebrows shot into her hair as she watched her friend squirm. When she'd agreed to come out tonight she thought they'd have a dance and a laugh and then stagger home. There was a chance they'd grill her about Cooper and she'd planned to tell them she didn't want to discuss him. She could not have predicted the arrival of George.

George slipped his finger around his collar. "Is it hot in here?"

"No, that's your guilt burning you up from the inside. Come on cousin! I've been very good and never asked you this around your mum, but what happened back then? I thought you were into Jordan. Then you went and scared her half to death after feeding her takeaway food."

"In his defence, he did spring for an ice cream." Jordan chimed in, adding to George's discomfort. Emily watched her glance longingly at the dance floor and back at Shelly, but their friend was oblivious. Shelly's attention was all on George and his confession, so Jordan was stuck.

"Fine! If you really must know, I'll tell you." He glared at Shelly. "You absolutely cannot tell anyone, though."

"I won't!"

"Do you promise?"

"Of course, you idiot. Hurry up and tell us the story."

"Okay. First of all," he looked across at Jordan, "I really did like you. I thought you were going to be fun to spend time with and I was looking forward to getting to know you better." She inclined her head as Emily watched on. "A week before we were due to go out I lost my job."

"What? Why didn't you say anything?"

"Shelly, please. You know our family. My mum would have not stopped nagging me until she was sure I'd found new employment. So, I just didn't tell her. But that meant I didn't have much cash on me and I couldn't ask to borrow any, because everyone would start asking questions." He turned to Emily to explain. "I have three brothers and a sister. So, lots of questions whenever something happens in your life.

"Anyway, my mate asked me if I could deliver a car to the person he'd sold it to. I've done this one or twice before and it's never been an issue. We normally meet somewhere in a carpark, I give him the keys and we're good. I get paid in cash to drop it off and everyone is happy."

"How much cash?" Jordan interrupted. "That envelope in your jacket was bulky."

"It's a fair amount of money. We would have had a great night." He grinned at her and she scowled. "Anyway, the drop off was at three o'clock. Plenty of time to get it done and get back to pick up Jordan in a taxi."

"Wait, the blue mustang wasn't even yours?" Jordan frowned again. "You had it at Shelly's engagement party when I met you." She looked at Emily. "That was part of the reason I went out with him; he had to have a car to be on the list, remember?

Emily laughed at the horrified look on Jordan's face. "The infamous list. You and Luke should get it printed on your invitations somehow when you get married."

"Ha! That's a great idea! Luke would totally go for that, too!"

"Oh, I heard you're getting married Jordan, congrats." George patted her hand and she slid it out of his reach and onto her lap.

"So, about that car. I'd borrowed it from my mate for the party. He has a couple of cars so it's no big deal to take one from time to time. I didn't feel like catching a taxi that day."

"You lying snake!" Shelly slapped him on the arm. "Everyone in the family thought that was your car." She turned to Jordan. "I'm sorry. I totally thought it was his."

Jordan laughed at her. "It's fine Shelly. It's old news. I couldn't care less about it."

"Yes, but you could have been killed that night." She turned back to George with a frown. "All because my cousin hides things from his family!"

"Do you want the story or not, Shelly? I could be dancing and meeting chicks right now, you know."

"If you don't hurry up and spit this story out I swear I'm going to dob you in to your dad!"

"Alright, keep your hair on." He rolled his eyes and finished the last of his beer. "So I'm meant to go at three. I know I'll be cashed up and have loads of time to get ready, but the deal changes at the last minute to nine o'clock and the location changes, too." He shook his head, thinking back to that night, trying to recall every detail to repeat to the women watching him now. "So now I'm in a panic. I don't have enough cash to take Jordan out and I'm expected somewhere at nine with the car."

The three women watched him intently, fascinated by his story as he hurried to finish. "I didn't want to cancel with you," he looked at Jordan, "but I couldn't ask you to pay for dinner and then let me rush off for thirty minutes in the middle. So I did the only thing I could think of. A quick dinner at the golden arches, followed by getting rid of the car, and then I would make it up to you by showing you a good time." He shrugged as he sat back in the booth. "I hoped we'd get along so well during dinner that you'd forgive that small bit of craziness and we'd laugh about it later. Those damn kids, though, throwing their pickles on the roof and making so much noise. I could see you were desperate to get out of there." He looked at Jordan again. "I'm really sorry. You were all dressed up and it would have been great if we'd made it to the casino before I managed to scare you off."

Emily laughed along with the details all through the story telling but all it did was remind her of Cooper. They weren't the only ones to have misunderstandings in a relationship. Jordan and George had much, much worse and that was on their one and only date. As the music blared around her and George continued to apologise, she finally admitted to herself her feelings for Cooper. She missed him. Any time she wasn't busy she wondered what he was doing, where he was working, and if he thought about her. She wondered what he was doing at this very moment…

Shelly's mouth still hung open from the last of George's revelations and Emily had an overwhelming urge to giggle. From the look on Jordan's face she did too. The music blared around them and George cleared his throat, looked at Shelly and inclined his head toward the bar. Before she moved and set him free she leaned in close, "I'm never setting you up with one of my friends again!"

CHAPTER 16

*E*mily groaned as she checked her email. Ed's new phone had turned out to be the bane of her life. Every time he got a bright idea he sent her a video. Today she planned to leave early and the last thing she needed was a new urgent task from Ed.

She clicked play and prepared herself for his newest message.

"Hi, Em! You're looking well." He laughed at his own joke and she resolved to steal his phone and hide it somewhere at tonight's Christmas party. "I know I'll see you tonight but I just wanted to touch base and let you know how pleased we are with the good work you've done in the last few months. Profits are up—now that we have a full complement of sales people again—and our future is looking bright." She smiled at the screen.

Finally, a message that's not accompanied by a tonne of work.

"Just one final thing, and I hope you're viewing this in private." His eyebrows rose and he gave her a meaningful look. "You know I like to meddle, right?"

Oh yes I do!

"Well, I need to let you know that I invited Cooper to the Christmas party and he accepted." He raised his hand on the screen. "I know! I know! You might not want to see him, but he wants to see you. You've seemed a bit sad lately and I can't help but think you would like a chance to see him and sort out what's happened. So, I've taken the situation into my own hands and I hope you won't mind. If you two need to apologise to each other, a Christmas party is a damn good place to do it.

"I hope we'll see you there Emily. We're rooting for you guys." He smiled a guilty smile and pushed the stop button. As she stared at his face frozen on the screen, she was reminded of that other video months ago when she'd had only a few minutes notice of Cooper's arrival. Now he was giving her just a few hours notice that she was going to see Cooper tonight.

This had to stop.

She pulled her phone toward her and punched in Ed's number on the speed dial. He picked up after just one ring and answered with an anxious tone, "Hello, Emily."

"Hi Ed. I guess you know why I'm calling."

"I hoped you wouldn't call. I hoped we'd just see you tonight." He sighed and she let him wallow in discomfort for a moment more. "My wife gave me an earful when I told her I invited Cooper."

"So she should. I will see you tonight and I do want to see Cooper, but I want to clear something up with you beforehand."

"Oh, what is it?" His tone brightened considerably at her words.

"This needs to be the very last time you interfere in my personal life. By continuing to push us together you are overstepping the boundaries of our professional relationship."

"I agree, and I'm sorry."

"You're sorry now that you know it's going to work out, but come on, Ed. If you did this to any other member of staff I'd be advising you that there could be legal action. It needs to stop."

"Okay, okay, I promise. No more meddling."

"From now on, only work-related meddling. That's something I can deal with"

"Yes, definitely only work related. I said I promised. Now I have to go and dress for tonight. We have quite a drive."

She hung up and stared at the phone, thinking about meeting Cooper in just a few hours. Goose bumps ran down her back as she thought about seeing him for the first time in weeks. She'd been frozen and indecisive, unsure what to do. She missed him, but the days had turned to weeks and she still hadn't called.

Tonight, she promised herself. Tonight we'll sort out what we are to each other.

~

*A*s Emily stepped through the double doors in the ballroom, her eyes drifted across the beautifully turned out crowd. The room was full of familiar faces, people she saw daily and some she only had contact with online. People waved to her and smiled and she returned the gesture as she scanned the faces.

She was looking for just one.

A hand touched her elbow and she turned to find herself face to face with him. The one who'd made every day seem fun while they'd conducted job interviews. Who'd manipulated every situation to ensure they spent time together. The man she'd spent so much time with and who she now could admit she missed like crazy.

He held out his hand and inclined his head toward the dance floor, a questioning look on his face.

Why not? Time to finish this once and for all.

He led her toward the throng of people who were gyrating to the latest dance hit and as they moved to the centre of the floor, the music magically changed to a mellower beat. She stepped into Cooper's arm and sighed as his hand snaked around her waist.

"You look beautiful."

"Thanks. I got a very nice pay rise thanks to you so I splurged on this dress."

"I wasn't talking about the dress, and your job had nothing to do with me and everything to do with you. Don't sell yourself short Emily. The way you've taken charge has been amazing." He smiled down at her as she tried to damp down the flurry of emotions swirling inside her.

"It's not quite the same without you in the office."

"Ahh… I hoped you'd miss me."

"I have missed you." She caught his eye and the sparkle of mischief there was unmistakeable. "You planned it this way, didn't you?"

"Maybe. I kind of hoped all those hours spent together week after week might tip the scales in my favour. My phone has remained mysteriously silent, however." He squeezed her hand and pulled her a little closer as they moved between the other couples.

"I wanted to call. I just wasn't sure that I should. I didn't know if you still felt the same way."

"I've always felt this way about you, from the first week we went out. You made it pretty clear to stay away, though. Both times." He smiled at her, a relaxed look that suited him. She snuggled closer, content in his arms.

"Want to hear something funny?"

"All I've had is funny, ever since I stepped into your office one innocent Tuesday morning. Between crazy job applicants, Andrew chewing me out, and my inability to come clean about my mother, what else have you got?"

"Oh this tops *all* of that."

"It tops being propositioned by one Lucy Jones during the interview?"

"It does."

"Better than resumes that smell like cheap sex candles have been dribbled all over them?"

"Much better." She laughed as he rattled off all the situations they'd found themselves in while they'd been on a mission to re-staff her company.

"Okay then. I'm all ears."

"You won't believe it, but we received an invoice this week for five hundred and twenty five dollars."

"And?"

"It was from Bill Gibbons."

Cooper searched his memory to put a face to that name. "Should I know who that is?"

"He's the guy we interviewed for the operations manager role. The only one as it turns out."

"Oh, I remember him. A surly and serious man. Kept going on about costs and keeping the staff on a short leash and didn't like it when you asked your questions."

"That's the one."

"Why would he send an invoice?"

"When he found out he didn't get the job after calling the office for weeks and weeks, he was so incensed that he decided to bill us for his time!"

"You're kidding."

"I wish I was. He charged us three hundred an hour and itemised it as an hour and a half for the interview and an extra hour for the time he'd spent calling us."

"Wow." Cooper laughed as they danced through the crowd. "Three hundred an hour? We couldn't afford him even if we had liked him. I think Simpsons has saved all the other companies from the worst job applicants in history." Emily laughed and his hand tightened around her waist. "How's my good friend Andrew, doing?"

"He's great. His feathers have all grown back."

"Has his vocabulary been extended in the last few months?" he looked down at her and she laughed at the meaning of his words.

"Maybe."

"I can just imagine what he can say now." He mimicked the parrot's voice, "Cooper is a liar! Cooper keeps secrets! Cooper might need counselling! And my all-time favourite, Cooper is banned from this house!" Emily laughed again and Cooper grinned his best white-toothed smile. "That bird hates me!"

"He doesn't hate you. He just has impeccable timing with his choice of phrases."

"I think he hates me."

"You'll have to come over and find out." She gazed at him, testing the waters, making sure they could find a way back to how they were before.

"Where are you living now, anyway? I exercised enormous self control and didn't badger Ed for any details."

"I moved in with Jordan and Luke while my place is being fixed up. Luke's house is enormous so I've been able to find my own space there. Andrew has new things to say, now, since Rex is quite taken with him and we are continually telling him to get away from the cage." She grinned. "I have to say Luke was just as upset as I was that we broke up again."

"Ahhh... my wingman was rooting for me. I bet he was disappointed that I stuffed it up."

"Can we sit down? I don't want to discuss this in the middle of the dance floor."

"Sorry, I promised myself I wouldn't bring it up."

She touched his face, not caring if anyone saw, "It's okay. I didn't mean I didn't want to talk about it. I meant I didn't want to talk about it here." She pulled away and tugged him through the crowd.

They left the dance floor but instead of sitting at a table she kept going, right back out the door she'd recently stepped through. The December night was warm and there was barely a breeze as Cooper followed her around the side of the building. Several bench seats glowed under an outdoor light and it was here that Emily planned to talk to him.

Before they reached the seats, a woman stepped out from behind a nearby tree. "Emily?" Emily stopped dead and then took a small step back. "Could we talk for a moment?"

"I don't think so Simone. You shouldn't be here."

"Who is that?" Cooper murmured close to her ear.

She turned slightly, her eyes not leaving the woman. "This is Simone, our ex sales manager's wife. The one who quit when he was let go." She gave her full attention back to the woman in front of her. "What do you want? I think Brett has done enough damage, don't you?"

"I want to apologise for what he did. He wasn't himself once he was unemployed and he struggled to find a new position. We had money problems and —"

"I don't really want to hear about it. I'm sorry, but you need to leave. Now." Emily took another step away and Cooper stepped in front of her, shielding her from Simone. "I didn't tell you this Cooper, but Brett appears to have started the fire. No one knows where he is."

"What?" he glanced over his shoulder and then back at Simone. "It's time you left. Can I see you to your car?"

"I just wanted to talk."

"It's probably better if you make an appointment. You can understand why this is awkward?" He indicated the car park, inviting her to lead the way. "I'll walk you to your car," he said, when she made no move.

"Okay, I'll leave. I won't make an appointment to see you Emily, but I just wanted you to know that I'm truly sorry for what he did. If I'd known I would have done everything to stop it."

Emily nodded as Simone finally let Cooper lead her away. She dropped onto the seat and gulped in big breaths of air. Her hands shook slightly as she watched for Cooper's return. When he didn't come back for several minutes, she decided to send security to look for him.

She'd only taken a few steps when Cooper appeared from around the corner of the building. "Oh thank God! I wondered where you were."

"Everything is fine. She started crying on the way to the car so I had a bit of a talk to her to calm her down. I assured her you knew she was sorry and that she had nothing to do with it."

"I can't believe she came here!"

"I know, but it's over now. I want all the gory details that I missed but right now my immediate concern is that she has put you on edge when I was getting close to confessing my undying love and devotion. If she's derailed my return to the good books I'll consider burning *her* house down as a thank you!"

Emily slapped him on the arm, "Don't you even joke about that."

"Sorry, I thought it could be too soon." He grinned and they walked slowly back to the seat.

Emily sat and indicated Cooper should sit too. "Okay, back to my carefully prepared speech." She grinned at him. "I thought about everything that you told me, and I want you to know that I forgive you for not telling me about your mother. I understand how that happened and why."

Cooper looked at his hands and fidgeted with his jacket. "I know I already said it, but I truly am sorry."

"I know. It was a misunderstanding that I should have just dealt with at the time."

"That goes double for me." He finally smiled and a trickle of excitement curled in Emily's stomach. She never could resist that surfer smile. "What do we do from here, though? Maybe I want a lot more than you can give."

"What do you want Cooper?"

"I want you to give me," he rolled his eyes at a himself, "what amounts to my third chance to get this right. I'm really not an odd person. This was my only secret—there's nothing else I need to tell you about. Not to be pushy, but if I had everything I wanted, I'd have you moved out of Luke's house and into mine by tomorrow." He grinned at her then, his usual confidence peeking through his reserved exterior.

"Can the bribe of a home by the beach work on you at this late stage?"

"Well, I do like the sound of the ocean when I wake up."

"Andrew would be happy there."

"Oh, Andrew. How will you handle him saying all those awful things to you?"

"I'll manage. We'll just have to teach him some new things to say." He reached across and took her hand, intertwining his fingers through hers. "I'm prepared to suffer a lifetime of him picking on me, if you'll say yes to us."

She licked her lips and his eyes darted to her tongue. Her anticipation at seeing him was nothing compared to the reality. She wanted nothing more than to let him back into her life, to be with him at his seaside apartment and wake up next to him each day. The weeks apart had shown her that no matter the hardships, or the complications, Cooper was the man she yearned for, the one she wanted to spend her life with.

"I'd be willing to say yes." Her eyes sparkled as she watched his trademark smile stretch across his face again. His fingers tightened on hers and he slid closer on the bench, wrapping his other arm around her shoulders.

She inclined her head and the excitement twisting in her stomach told her this was right for them. Exactly what was needed.

His lips pressed against hers, gentle at first, then becoming more insistent. She wrapped her hands around his neck and twisted her fingers in the back of his hair. Her fierce flare of longing surprised her as his tongue made all the promises she'd hoped for.

When he pulled away he rested his forehead against hers. "I love you Emily. I have for ages and I should have told you sooner."

She put her finger against his lips to shush him. "We have our whole lives to make up for that. Our whole lives to love each other."

"I intend to take full advantage, starting tonight." He looked back at the house, the sound of the party wafting across the grass to them. "How long do you think we have to stay here before we can escape?"

EPILOGUE

"*L*uke, can I help you with that, buddy?"

"Nope, I'm good. I help people move house all the time. Ask Jordan. I wooed her family with my moving skills long before I managed to convince her to let me into her heart."

Cooper laughed and slapped him on the back. "You're such a romantic. It's a refreshing change."

"All I know is I knew she was the one for me, almost from day one."

"I know exactly how that feels. Looks like we both managed to make good."

Luke put down the two boxes he'd been carrying. "Jordan says I'm to remind you that we'll hunt you down and kill you if you mess up again. So consider that message delivered from my fiancée!"

Cooper feigned fear and took a step back. "Message received! Don't worry, I've learned my lesson. We're going to be happy together, especially once I get her to agree to marry me."

Luke clapped him on the back. "You're proposing?"

"I just might be."

"I'm pleased to hear it. Can you sow the idea of a double wedding when you pop the question? Jordan won't let me set a concrete date and I've always wanted to go to a double wedding. Maybe we can make it happen." His bright eyes made Cooper laugh.

"You're making all of Emily's man-crush jokes seem not so funny right now, but I'll do my best. The main thing is that my bride is happy on the day—I couldn't care less how that happens."

"I know that, man. I can see how much you love her. How the hell are you gonna put up with that bird, though?"

As he spoke Andrew started up in the corner. "Get down Rex! Coooooooperrrrrrrr sucks!" He'd taken to saying that in a disparaging tone which added to the hilarity. "Coooooooperrrrrrrr is poop. Rex, down! Coooooooperrrrrrrr did it again!"

"I'd have his blanket over his cage twenty four hours a day." Luke said with a shake of his head. "I'll go get some more boxes."

Emily carried a bag of clothing to their room before she came out to talk to the parrot. "Andrew, what did I tell you about being mean to Cooper?"

"Cooper sucks!" She sighed, as she got ready to

place the blanket and growled at him, "I taught you new words. Why don't you say any of those?"

"Don't," the target of his abuse said behind her. "Let him be. It's not his fault."

"I'm really sorry. We'll teach him new things to say, I promise."

Cooper wrapped his arms around her waist and pulled her close. "I know we will. I'm looking forward to brainwashing him to say bad stuff. I work from home when I'm not consulting, remember? He'll be at my mercy all day." He laughed and she put her head on his shoulder, watching the waves break across the road, content to be moving in with him today. His hand caressed her hair and she shivered, knowing the things he'd whispered to her earlier would all take place once Jordan and Luke left. Lucky she didn't have a lot to move—most of her belongings had been destroyed or damaged in the fire.

She turned around in Cooper's arms and looked at Andrew again, before reaching out and giving him a seed. He took it from her hand and held it in one claw before he said, "Coooooperrrrrrrr has my heart."

The End

SNEAK PEEK TICKET TO RIDE

I hope you enjoyed Adventures In Hiring. I loved every moment of writing it and I'm thrilled the series has been so well received by my readers. I hope you'll continue along and find out where these whacky characters find themselves!

To keep the love and laughter going, here's a sneak peek of book four - Ticket to Ride. Here's what you can expect:

Stuck in a terrifying position. With the one guy she can't stand!

Jenny Blake is the new HR Manager at Simpson Stationery. Her old boss, Emily, is now in charge of Simpsons and every day at her perfect job is bliss. As the women of the office guess over when Emily's boyfriend Cooper will propose to her, Emily wins a prize that will change lives.

Mack Harrison leads a simple life as a baker. He creates edible masterpieces, experiments with icing swirls and spends his spare time with his family. When Jenny is forced to order a cake from his store, his previous awful first impressions don't help him win her over.

A series of mix-ups see Jenny and Mack on opposite sides of one huge misunderstanding. As they continue to 'bump' into each other, Jenny's animosity grows.

Until that unexpected event that Emily set in motion throws them together.

Now Jenny is wondering - does she have a stalker? Or is fate throwing them together? Will a life-threatening situation help her to see the good in Mack? Or will she wish for a bolt of lightning to shoot him off the rollercoaster of love?

Set against a backdrop of weddings, furry friends and the characters you've come to love, Ticket To Ride is the most fun you'll have on a romance rollercoaster!

Make sure you don't miss it!

Ticket To Ride

"Shh... here she comes! Hide that paper."

Emily narrowed her eyes at the group of women gathered around the reception desk at Simpson Stationery so early in the morning. "What are you ladies up to?"

"Oh, nothing. Just catching up on what we did on our days off, comparing New Year's Eve notes." Jenny stepped forward with a smile, "Did you do anything interesting?"

"Hmm... just the usual. Cooper and I relaxed at the beach. Andrew picked on him as much as I let him. Oh, he bought me this for Christmas." She held out her hand and Jenny and the other girls squealed.

"Oh my gosh! Is that all diamonds?"

"That must have cost him a fortune!"

"It's beautiful."

She pulled the bracelet up to admire it, the same as she had every day since Cooper had presented it with a flourish on Christmas morning. He'd gone overboard with his first Christmas gift, and she'd almost felt guilty that she'd bought him a diving watch he could wear while surfing. Sure, it was beautiful quality and she'd had it engraved, but a diamond bracelet felt particularly opulent.

"You didn't wear that between Christmas and New Year's when we were here in the office. We would have noticed."

"I put it carefully away, but Cooper got cranky. He said it was everyday jewellery, not only for special occasions. I'm terrified I'll lose it, actually." She examined the clasp for the hundredth time and ran her finger over the closure. "He insists I wear it."

"If you need someone to look after it, I'm available." Fiona held up her own bare wrist and laughed. "It would be a sacrifice, but I'm up for the challenge."

"I'll keep that in mind."

"Time to get back to work, I guess." Jenny picked up her handbag and turned toward the stairs. "We better look busy, ladies—don't want the new HR manager telling us off." Jenny waved her hands above her head as the rest of the women laughed.

"I guess that includes me. Don't want to get myself a written warning on the first day back in the new year." Emily laughed as she followed Jenny up the stairs. When they both reached the top, they fell in step together. "What were you all whispering about down there?"

"Don't tell them I told you, but they're taking bets on whether Cooper will make an honest woman of you," Jenny giggled as she reached her office and opened the door. Her eyes settled on the small burnished sign with the title of Human Resources Manager and pride flickered for a moment. She stepped through the doorway with a grin. "They're all carrying on like it's a sure thing."

"Are they just?"

"Yeah, sorry. I should have gotten them to stop, but it seems harmless enough."

"Who is betting he'll do it the soonest?"

"That would be Casey. She was convinced he would propose at Christmas, but her second choice was New Year's Eve."

"They barely know Cooper; how could they guess what's on his mind?"

"He made quite an impact in the months he worked here. The girls swooned every day when he arrived. I'm sure one of them would have asked him out if it hadn't been so obvious that he only had eyes for you."

"I tried so hard to keep it a secret." Emily frowned and rested her hip against the door frame.

"Well, I'm not sure there's ever been a worse fail in the history of office romances. The day you carried Andrew out to the car and he was screaming how Cooper broke your heart was quite an eye-opener for everyone." Jenny switched on her computer and sat in her chair as she began to laugh. "I can still remember the screeching carrying up the stairs and Cooper's eyes as wide as saucers. I may never forget that."

"Oh, funny." Emily stepped into the room and flopped down in one of Jenny's visitor chairs. She unzipped the side of her handbag and slipped her fingers into the small compartment. "Did you join in and have a guess about when Cooper might propose?"

"Not officially, but if I'd paid my money, I'd have chosen New Year's Eve, too." She leaned back and stared at Emily. "I'm sorry; it must be awkward to talk about it. We're being silly. I won't mention it again."

"It's okay. You should have thrown your money into the pot," she said as she placed her sparkling diamond on Jenny's keyboard.

A few moments of silence settled on the room as Jenny stared at the stone, her brain slowly making the connection about what it meant. As realisation dawned, she jumped up from her seat, letting out a scream of excitement.

"Oh my God, he did it! He did it! Congratulations! I can't believe you don't have a ring!" She ran around the desk and hugged Emily tightly. "Did you set a date? How did he propose?"

Emily laughed at her excitement. "Wow. You're nearly as excited as my friends were."

"I knew it! I knew he was madly in love with you and wouldn't wait too long." Before she could say anything else, Casey's face appeared in the doorway.

"Everything okay, you two?" Her eyes widened as she watched Emily click the ring box closed. "Is that what I think it is?" she shrieked.

"Not quite, but it means the same thing," Emily laughed. "I hear you might have won the sweep."

Casey doubled over with laughter as she fell into the room. "I knew it!"

"That's what I said." Jenny moved back behind her desk.

"Bet you wish you paid your money now. I just made three hundred dollars!" She high-fived Emily. "Thank you, Cooper!"

"Three hundred? How many of you had a guess?"

"Almost everyone, except Jenny. The warehouse guys were in it, too. I was the only one who chose the holidays, though. Most of the guys chose much later in the year. A sales guy who shall remain nameless said it would be years before Cooper would commit and give up his freedom. Wait until I rub this in his face!" She chuckled as she sped from the room to spread the news. Emily rolled her eyes and stood.

"Well, time to check my millions of emails. Thanks for the early morning entertainment."

"You're welcome. Get ready for a steady stream of congratulations today."

Ticket To Ride is available now at the store where you purchased this book. Order your copy so you don't miss out!

I always hate waiting for new books in a series to be released, so while you're waiting, here's a sneak peek of book one in my Famous Love series, *Contracted For Love*. Here's what you can expect:

Two people. Total strangers. Asked to convince the world that they're in love

Imagine if your favourite engaged celebrities weren't really in love. Imagine if their relationship was cooked up to boost their careers. What if everything was fake? From the holidays, the public romance, right down to the bedroom antics?

That's exactly what you'll discover in Contracted For Love.

Potty-mouthed Charlotte Shipton and child-star Jack Fawkner strike a deal when both put their signatures to an unlikely, and top secret, marriage contract. She'll rise through the unknown ranks in Hollywood. He'll show the world he's left behind his tap-dancing child-star days. Together, they'll set the world's hearts on fire, while ignoring their own secret desires.

Only time will tell if the truth will tear them apart, or if their secret will stay locked away, along with the contract.

Contracted For Love is a roller coaster ride of crazy activity, from the first moment they meet, to their Paris vacation under the gaze of the media and the constant pressures of a famous rockstar and his crazy bandmates. You'll laugh out loud as Charlotte makes her mark on Jack Fawkner and his heart!

Contracted For Love

"What. The. Actual. Fuck?"

Charlotte Shipton stood open-mouthed as she stared at Jack Fawkner across the conference room table. His fat, balding manager, Freddy Caspian, was grinning like an idiot who'd just won the lotto and would be broke within a month. Her own partner in crime, Jay Stevens, was grinning just as widely, which was the part she couldn't actually believe. "Did you really just say you think we should get married, Jay? The two of us," she indicated herself and Jack, "who just met," she checked her iPhone with the push of the home key, "seventeen minutes ago?"

"Charlotte, calm down. Let me explain why this is such a good idea."

"This is not a fucking good idea, Jay."

"You were right about the potty mouth," Freddy said quietly, to no one in particular. Jay sighed and glared at him.

"A fucking potty mouth? That's what you think I have? I can tell you, Mr. Fat Fuck, that I have so much more where that came from that it's not even funny." She crossed her arms across her ample chest and glared at him, daring him to say another word. He finally looked away and she turned her icy stare on Jack. "Did you know about this bullshit?"

Jack put his hands up, as though to ward off the sun. "Woah, don't turn your spotlight on me. I'm hearing this for the first time, too." He turned to Freddy. "What were you thinking? Why would I want to marry *her*?" he flicked his head at Charlotte dismissively.

Jay piped up before Jack's agent could say anything. "Freddy and I have discussed it and we think it could work really well for both of your careers."

Charlotte shot out of her chair, making it fall over with a crash. "Since when do you have discussions of this magnitude without me? What are you, my fucking pimp, now? You're arranging marriages for me? If not him, would you have had someone else lined up to take his place, Jay?"

Jack watched her with interest. He'd heard whispers of a feisty Australian who'd recently shown up in Hollywood, and now here she was in front of him, living up to every story he'd heard. The gossip had been spot-on for once. Her eyes were flashing and her sun-kissed, blonde hair flailed around behind her whenever she flounced around the room. She was a ball of furious energy, right now. In Los Angeles, everyone seemed so fake that, even with her crazy temper, it was refreshing to see someone being themselves and being totally honest with everyone in the room. There was no way he wanted to marry her, though.

"Charlotte, this could make a huge difference to your career. You're having trouble getting those great roles, but being married to someone who's been in the business for as long as Jack has will give you the credibility you need to get more auditions. It's a huge foot in the door. I know you'll be a great actress, but you need to get your name known in the papers. If that's not through acting, then we need to find another way. This is a perfect option."

"Wait," Jack finally spoke up. "What am I getting out of this? Why do I have to be her meal ticket?"

"You're not my fucking meal ticket, asshole.

There's not a hope in hell of me marrying your high-and-mighty ass." She glared at him and he glared straight back.

"Why are you calling me an asshole? We just met. You could at least save that for after we're married, sweetheart."

Charlotte let out a scream of frustration and spun around to look out the window. She could feel tears of fury pricking the corners of her eyes, but she'd be damned if she'd let them think she was crying. She contemplated hurling her agent out of this twenty-six story window, if she could get it open, but she would not cry real tears.

Freddy addressed Jack in his most conciliatory tone. "What you get out of this Jack, is a marriage that makes you seem older in the eyes of the public. You've been out of the spotlight for a while, but you're still a big star. We've been trying to shed that childish good-boy image and this is as quick way to lift your music career out of the teeny-bopper stage and into the big-time."

"I don't need to get married to do that. My music isn't for kids."

"We know that, but so far, they don't. The kids are your fans, and adults think of you as their children's crush. No one has quite worked out that you've grown up, yet. You're fairly clean-cut, so unless you're planning a bender in Vegas, or to woo a Kardashian, this is the next best thing."

"Well, I do prefer brunettes." Charlotte snorted from the other side of the room, where she gazed out over the city. "Regardless, it sounds like a bad idea. When word gets out..."

"Word won't get out," Jay interrupted. "It can't. We'll have an ironclad contract for you both to sign and you'll be sworn to secrecy. The only people who will know about this are in this room, and all of us stand to benefit from this going off without a hitch —pardon the wedding pun." He smirked at his joke, as Charlotte spun around from the window, wide-eyed.

"We wouldn't even tell our own family?"

"No. It'd have to be an absolute secret. There's too much chance of this getting out, if you tell anyone, and the scandal would most likely have the exact opposite effect on your careers."

"Although, it might help, you never can tell..."

"Don't even think about it, Freddy. You're not leaking this shit to the press. How desperate do you think that will make me look?" Jack glared at his manager, daring him to continue.

"You're right: bad idea. Stick with the wedding."

"There's not going to be a fucking wedding, you morons." Charlotte shouted at the three of them. "Why would I marry a washed-up child star? He's nearly ten years older than me!"

"Why would I marry someone who can't speak a single sentence without cursing? Are you sure you're an actress, honey? Can't you act like a lady for a few minutes?"

"Fuck you, *Jackie* Fawkner." She put the emphasis on his old acting name that had followed him around since he was seven. "You're a grown-up, now, kiddo: you're allowed to swear whenever you want."

"Pleased to see that you know who I am, even if I've never heard of you."

She raised her middle finger to him and held it in front of her with a fake smile. Jack shook his head and returned his attention to Freddy. "You'll get married because you're in love, of course!" He clapped his hands together in glee. "You met and it was an instant attraction. We'll have you go out for a couple of dinner dates, and maybe to a theme park, and then, voila, a wedding announcement! Charlotte, you'll gush about his manly abs and how you love his grown-up music." She snorted and made vomiting sounds as Freddy turned to Jack. "You have a crazy attraction to her free-spirited ways and her complete refusal to be intimidated by Hollywood or conform to the usual expectations. You get to marry a smoking-hot woman, and this will have your female fans taking notice of what's now gone off the market. It's genius—very adult."

"Except that he prefers brunettes, dickhead. Have you thought about what you're saying? How long do you expect this charade to go on for?" Charlotte looked at all of them, horrified that they hadn't already dismissed this insane idea. Jay cleared his throat, as though he'd thought this wouldn't have come up so early. Charlotte glared at him and crossed her arms again. "How fucking long, Jay?"

"We think three years is a reasonable time frame." He said, waiting for the explosion that was sure to follow. Amazingly, Charlotte stood in total silence, absolutely stunned, judging by the look on her face.

It was Jack who spoke up first. "Three years? We have to be married for three years? How the hell will I put up with her for that long? We haven't even been here for three hours and I already have a headache."

"You have a headache? I thought you were a rock star?" Charlotte turned to Jay, "Do you want me to marry him because he's gay?" She turned back to Jack. "Are you gay, Jack? Because again, you're an adult and you don't have to hide that shit, anymore. Just be yourself dude."

"Really?" he looked at her in disgust.

"Really," she said with another fake smile and a nod to show that she meant it.

"How would we explain living apart?" Jack asked Freddy. Jack's manager glanced at Jay, wondering if they'd even discussed that when they had hatched this plan last night over a bottle of Jack Daniels.

"That's easy: you're gay." Charlotte threw in helpfully.

"Would you shut up?" he glared at her.

"Charlotte, please don't get mad," he glanced at her before he continued, "The only way this can work is if you're married for all intents and purposes. You'd need to live together, shop together, vacation together—it's all or nothing. There's no other way to make it work in this age of social media and instant news. You can't half-ass it or the secret will be out in the first week."

Jack and Charlotte stared at each other as the details of this crazy arrangement sank in. She blinked once and dropped into the nearest chair, all the fight shocked out of her. "Let me get this straight in my poor, *blonde* brain," she glared at Jack before she went on. "You want us to have a fake engagement, move in together, have a fake wedding, actually include our families in the lies and not tell them that they are feeling happy for a fake future we'll never have… and you want us to do it for three years?"

"That about sums it up."

"What. The. Actual. Fuck?"

Contracted For Love is available now at the store where you purchased this book. Order your copy so you don't miss out!

ALSO BY TRACEY PEDERSEN

Finding Sweet Love Series

All At Sea

All Afloat

All Adrift

All Ashore

All About Us

One Week Love Story Series

Seven Days To Me

Seven Days To Us

Married This Year Series

Married This Year

Simmering Love

Adventures In Hiring

Ticket To Ride

She's Having A Baby

Married This Christmas

Men About Town Series

Tap That!

Tempt Me!

Tight Ass!

Thigh High!

Turned On!

Tinsel Time!

Famous Love Series

Contracted For Love

Contracted For Life

Secure My Heart Series

Track

The Secret Billionaire's Club Series

The Billionaire's Heart

The Billionaire's Luck

The Billionaire's Treat

The Billionaire's Duty

The Billionaire's Spark

The Billionaire's Club

The Billionaire's Scare

The Billionaire's Feast

The Billionaire's Gift

The Billionaire's Surprise

Standalone Books

Vermont Christmas

Available from your favourite online retailer!

ABOUT THE AUTHOR

Tracey Pedersen is an Australian author who has finally accepted she is meant to write, write, write! In 2016 she released her first romance, a series of non-fiction titles, and six books under a separate pen name. Now writing full time, and fighting the urge to write every second of the day, she loves travel, crocheting, scrapbooking, replying to reader emails and spending WAY too much time on Facebook!

If you enjoy romantic stories that mimic real life, with an extra twist thrown in, you'll love Tracey's books. She enjoys dialogue that sounds exactly like we all talk and weaving travel into her stories too. A few laughs don't go astray either!

FOLLOW TRACEY ONLINE

I love to hear from readers so don't be shy, look me up!

Check out my author page on the site where you purchased this book to buy other books in this series. There are plenty of other goodies for you to choose from in both paperback and eBook.

Visit my website below to join my mailing list and receive advance notice of new releases, giveaways, and other secret bonuses exclusively for subscribers.

As a special thank you, you can get free books there too!

For more information...
www.traceypedersen.com

WANT TO HANG OUT WITH ME?

Join my reader group on Facebook!

facebook.com/groups/TPSFunHouse/

- facebook.com/TraceyPedersen
- twitter.com/TraceyLPedersen
- instagram.com/traceypedersenauthor
- bookbub.com/profile/tracey-pedersen